Chosen by Chigs

Galactic Pirate Brides

Book Six

Tamsin Ley

Twin Leaf Press

All characters in this book, be they alien, human, or something else entirely, are the product of the author's imagination. Any resemblance to actual people, situations, or events are entirely coincidental.

No part of this book may be reproduced, transmitted, or distributed in any form or by any means without explicit written permission from the author, with the exception of brief quotes for use in reviews, articles, or blogs. This book is licensed for your enjoyment only. Thank you a million zillion hearts and kisses for purchasing.

Cover by The Book Brander

Paperback version
ISBN-13: 978-1-950027-86-6
Copyright © 2024 Twin Leaf Press
All rights reserved.

Twin Leaf Press
PO Box 672255
Chugiak, AK 99567

Chapter One

Chigs stood motionless beside the sterile med bay cot, his face a hardened mask as he stared down at the copper-skinned denaidan woman. Beside him, Tovik shuffled his feet, the usual youthful mirth drained from his face.

Across the cot, Mek, the ship's doctor, pulled the retractable arm of the med bay scanner out of the way, his usually clean-shaven face dark with several days of stubble. "Her neural pathways are fried, just like the others. Dollard's experiments left nothing but husks."

Chigs's fists clenched involuntarily, feeling the weight of a thousand lost futures in the quiet rise and fall of the woman's breath. *Ellam Cua, how could you allow this to happen? To give us such hope, only to tear it away so cruelly?*

Though her chest rose and fell, beneath her closed eyelids there was no flicker of consciousness, no trace of what should be a vibrant animating spirit. Several more women, like this one, had been returned to cryopods, awaiting a decision on what should be done.

"I thought we'd found our future." Tovik's voice hitched. "We only saved bodies, not lives. Not mates."

A heavy silence settled between them, broken only by the relentless beep of the vital monitors.

"There has to be a way to reach them," Chigs insisted. "We can't abandon them to this empty existence." He refused to give up, not when the nagging urge to locate his destined mate had become his singular driving force. Other males had discovered mates among the human women on their crew, but to Chigs, humans had always seemed too small, too fragile, to offer him a viable bed partner.

Mek sighed, his dark eyes clouded with resignation. "I'll keep digging into the lab data, but we need to face reality. The odds of them ever waking are almost nil."

Tovik turned away morosely. "I'll get cryopod ready so she can rest with the others."

Feeling useless, Chigs retreated with heavy footsteps, the corridors of the *Icarus* stretching out before him like the tunnels of some ancient crypt. His quarters offered little relief, the spacious confines now seeming too tight, too suffocating. He'd never had such lush accommodations in his life, but the captured Syndicorp flagship had enough officers' quarters on board for each rebel to have their own suite. The *Icarus*—with its advanced technology, size, and weaponry—had become a floating base for the entire rebellion in their fight against the corporation that ruled the galaxy, and they'd executed several successful raids on Syndicorp facilities in the past few weeks.

Chigs had believed finding the denaidan females was an answer to their prayers; Syndicorp had exterminated all life on their home planet, and his species had believed their females were extinct. But instead of lighting divine hope among the rebels, the brain-dead women only served as a reminder for all that had been lost.

Chigs peered longingly at his rumpled bed, glimpsing his eyes, bloodshot with blue veins, in the mirror across the way. He needed to sleep, but dreaded the nightmares of women in cryopods that had been haunting him every night. He'd believed they were a sign he was destined to find his mate. Now, he could only think his god was playing tricks on him. Collapsing onto the edge of his bunk, he cradled his head in his copper-skinned hands. Deep breaths failed to ease the throbbing ache spreading through his skull.

"Ellam Cua, stop this torture." He murmured, praying that somewhere in the vastness of space, his deity was listening.

With a sigh, he lay back and closed his eyes, surrendering to the lull of sleep...

Devastation and decay surrounded Chigs, like the remnants of a city lost in time. Ahead, a dusty road faded into mist. His gorge rose in dreadful anticipation. He didn't want to be here. Didn't want to see this nightmare again. Yet his body felt numb as he glided forward on unmoving legs, the insistent breeze nudging him along until the road transformed into a long corridor with metal floors and pale, sterile walls. Rows of translucent, pod-like chambers caged him on either side. Harsh lighting glinted off the pods, hiding the contents, but he already knew what lay within.

His hearts pounded like twin fists in his chest, his mouth dry as sand as he tried to turn aside. Yet he was compelled to peer inside the nearest one. The copper-colored skin, perfect breasts, and curved hips of a denaidan female lay motionless behind the glass. Tubes and wires coiled around her like malevolent sea creatures. Her open eyes seemed to stare back at him with accusation.

He wanted to help her. To free her. But his movements weren't his own. He moved to the next pod and the next, each one holding another female. Some resembled his mother, his aunt, his cousins, all long dead; lost in the destruction of his planet.

Through the mist, a familiar feminine voice whispered his name, the sound caressing his senses like a lover's touch. He spun, searching for the source. So many pods. How was he supposed to find her? Yearning and anguish entwined his heart as he moved down the rows.

A bark of hoarse, male laughter echoed through the room, harsh and grating. Although Chigs had never met Dr. Dollard in person, he was certain that's who the laughter belonged to—the scientist responsible for the atrocities committed against his people.

Rage burning in his gut like molten lead, Chigs whirled, bellowing, "You're dead!" His voice reverberated off the sterile walls.

"You'll never find her," the voice cackled, mocking him. "Never..."

Chigs woke with a start, covered in sweat and breathing hard. Dollard's laughter still echoed in his mind as he swung his legs over the edge of the bed and sat, blinking to clear his vision. His quarters held the familiar scents of oil and steel, a sharp contrast to the antiseptic stench of the lab from his dream. He dragged a hand over his face and down his beard.

The dream had been the same for the past three nights. Why did the lab feel so familiar? It wasn't the lab from the raid, and yet he felt like he'd been there before. Although the dream's details were already fuzzing around the edges, the horror of the translucent pods and the women imprisoned within them continued to sting like razor cuts to his soul.

He rose and began pacing again, unable to silence Dollard's laughter in his head.

"That evil *qumli's* dead," Chigs muttered out loud.

During the most recent raid, Dollard had been swept into the vacuum of space without a suit, which no ordinary human could've survived. But Dollard's twisted experiments might have granted him unnatural resilience, and Rust hadn't been able to find a body. The human had cheated death before. Could he do it again? Ellam Cua was a trickster god, and would appreciate such a twist.

Shaking his head, Chigs resumed pacing. Regardless of whether Dollard was dead or alive, the raid on his lab hadn't been a complete success. Several shuttles had escaped, presumably carrying cryopods and more denaidan females with them—females who could still be alive.

Not for long if someone continues Dollard's experiments.

Chigs cursed, slamming a fist into the wall. The polymer panel dented under the blow, and pain lanced up his arm. But physical pain was nothing compared to the anguish of knowing there were more females out there, unreachable, untraceable. Was he doomed to hear that voice in his dreams for the rest of his life? She felt so real, like they were connected. He almost felt—

Chigs froze mid-pace, hearts pounding. What if the lab he was seeing wasn't the one they'd already raided? The female voice calling his name floated through his memory once more, like a song barely heard on a breeze.

My mate.

It had to be. Only mate bonds allowed couples to communicate through thoughts. And he felt certain that a female in that lab was calling him to rescue her. She was meant to be his. The realization felt like a star going nova, staggering in its implications.

But how was he supposed to find her? He needed more clues. Coordinates. A map. Anything!

Chigs closed his eyes and bowed his head. "Ellam Cua, I don't understand. Please. Show me the path to my mate."

Silence filled his quarters. No booming voice came down to give him divine orders. But after a long moment, his mind conjured the image of liquid brown eyes that softened into a smooth pale face with round cheeks and a gentle smile.

Emmy?

Chigs frowned. The human female had joined the rebellion almost a cycle ago, but he'd never paid her much mind. She was small and easy to overlook, even for her species. But he knew crew members sometimes sought her out to speak of personal troubles or ask for advice. Now he wondered... could she be some kind of spiritual guide?

The more he considered it, the more certain he became. Was it possible that Ellam Cua wanted him to seek Emmy out and ask for her help interpreting his calling? Maybe she would show him the path to his mate.

Chigs smiled as determination burned away his earlier helplessness. Those CEOs at Syndicorp would soon regret the day they'd dared to cross a denaidan on a mission for his mate. He'd find the lab. Rescue every last woman. And burn Dollard and any of his remaining experiments to dust.

Chapter Two

Emmy entered her office and set an empty box on the edge of her desk. Brushing a stray curl of brown hair from her eyes, she turned and surveyed the room. Her new office on board the *Icarus* was everything she'd always dreamed of, with a comfortable dovegray sofa and matching chairs for her counseling sessions and mellow ambient lighting. A meditation fountain trickled gently in the corner, and she'd even managed to get her hands on a potted plant of unknown species with long, greenish-blue fronds. If she didn't know better, she'd never guess they were on board a spaceship.

Her gaze settled on a shelf holding the small plush toys she'd brought with her when she'd fled Aleigh. These were the only things that were out of place. She picked up an orange and yellow octopus with soft, floppy tentacles, remembering one of her younger patients counting down fears on each of the creature's arms. She'd kept the toys as a reminder of her patients' successes, but it was becoming clear that her previous counseling methods had no use among the hardened members of the rebellion. Just yesterday, Rust had ripped the wings off her plush dragon before stalking out in anger.

She placed the octopus into the storage box and picked up a soft lavender netorpok with a long tail, tucking it into the box too. "You gotta go, guys. Sorry."

A hard knock on her office door interrupted her momentary nostalgia. Had Rust come back? Though he had obvious anger issues, she didn't think he'd ever hurt her, but she wasn't sure her poor stuffed animals were up for another visit. Voice tight, she called, "Come in?"

The door slid open to reveal Chigs, one of the denaidan fighters from Kashatok's crew. His braided hair brushed the top of the door frame, and he wore black pants and a white shirt rolled up at the sleeves to reveal the corded muscles beneath his coppery forearms. She'd only spoken to him in passing, but today a strange urgency had replaced his usual unsociability.

"Are you busy?" Uncertainty laced his deep voice.

"Not at all. What can I help you with, Chigs?" She moved around the desk to smile at the big denaidan male.

His copper eyes flickered from her to the remaining stuffed animals on her shelf. "Those are interesting totems."

Emmy blinked, surprised by his assumption. "They aren't totems. Just... toys. For comfort and therapy."

"Therapy?" Chigs raised an eyebrow, clearly puzzled.

Emmy's cheeks warmed. He obviously had no idea what her profession was about. "I'm a psychologist. I help people understand their thoughts and feelings." She let out a breath. "Or at least I used to."

"My error," Chigs muttered, his cheeks flushing a deep blue green. "The way Mek refers to you, I thought you were, well..." He shifted his weight uncomfortably. "Some sort of mystic."

Emmy's heart gave a pang at the mention of Mek's name. He'd been the latest in a string of heartbreaks that had made her swear off relationships. *There was no relationship, Emmy,* she chided herself. Mek had never returned her feelings, no matter how much she hoped he might. His heart had always been meant for another...

She shook off her current line of thinking. Chigs was here for her counsel, not to watch her wallow in regrets.

Forcing a smile, she said, "No harm done. Is there something specific you'd like to talk about?"

Chigs took a single step forward so the door could slide closed behind him. "Can you interpret dreams?"

The intense way his copper eyes connected with hers made Emmy's breath catch in her throat. It felt like the room suddenly became a few degrees warmer. Why did all the denaidan rebels have to be so damn hot?

Get a grip, Emmy. She'd literally just reminded herself to keep it professional, and here she was, letting her hormones drag her around again.

She cleared her throat. "I'd be happy to listen and offer my insights." She gestured to the couch across from her. "Please, sit."

Chigs strode toward the seating area, the sheer size of his chiseled body making Emmy feel even more petite than usual. He sat with his back to the shelf of stuffed animals, knees apart in a way that seemed to dominate the space. Jaw clenching and unclenching, he stared at the floor for a moment.

Emmy sat in the chair opposite and waited for him to gather his thoughts. Waiting and silence were important parts of the psychological process, allowing the client to open up in their own time. But she was finding it difficult to keep her mind off the muscular breadth of his shoulders or the thickness of his massive thighs.

After another moment, Chigs leaned forward and rested his elbows on his knees. "I keep having a dream about a laboratory filled with denaidan women in cryopods."

Emmy's heart squeezed. Discovering that Syndicorp had been holding denaidan females captive for breeding—especially after everyone had assumed there were no females left—had been a horrific shock, especially for the denaidan males. She was surprised more crew members hadn't visited her office. "That's perfectly understandable," she said gently. "Dreams are often the subconscious mind's way of processing trauma. Talking about your feelings may help stop the nightmares."

Chigs's hands clenched into fists, knuckles bleaching under his burnished skin. "I don't need to stop the dreams. I need to focus on them so I can rescue those women." His gaze on hers intensified, the desperation in his eyes burning like twin copper lasers. "My mate is with them, I know it. Ellam Cua is trying to show me how to save her."

Now his question about her being a mystic made more sense—Chigs believed his dream was a vision from his god. "Chigs," she began cautiously, "I know dreams can feel incredibly real, but—"

"You were in the dream," he interrupted. "You're the key to helping me interpret it. The key to finding my mate."

Her chest tightened. His devotion to a mate who might not even exist was inspiring, though she couldn't help acknowledging the tiny, sharp prick of jealousy she felt. She wanted to help him, even if all she could do was ease his mind. "Okay," she said, folding her hands on her lap. "Let's explore your dream further. Tell me more."

Taking a deep breath, he began telling her about the lab. When he described translucent chambers, a flash of guilt made her guts twist with nausea as she recalled the face of one of her patients. Syndicorp had been testing methods of rewiring synapses to remove violent tendencies in criminals. The project had sounded good in theory, but the test subjects all suffered severe memory loss and impaired cognition. She'd left Syndicorp because of chambers just like those. Now Chigs was dreaming of them? She couldn't take back what she'd done, but she'd do everything in her power to prevent anyone else from suffering. Shaking off her thoughts, she focused on what Chigs was saying.

"The worst part of the dream is when I hear Dr. Dollard laughing," Chigs finished through gritted teeth. "I worry he's still out there somewhere. That bastard will never give up."

Emmy shook her head and spoke in a firm voice. "Dollard is dead. Humans aren't like denaidans. Like most species, we don't last long in space without a suit."

Chigs growled—literally growled—before saying, "He escaped death before. He could do it again."

Emmy's gaze flickered to the empty spot on her shelf where the stuffed toy Rust had shredded once sat. The volatile cyborg had been struggling with doubts about Dollard when he lost control. Perhaps she should take a step back and reassess the situation with Chigs before pursuing this topic. Besides, there was another thing eating at the edges of her mind. "Chigs, did you work for Syndicorp?"

His features hardened with loathing. "Yes. Like most of my *iluq*, I was a trooper."

"Perhaps what is manifesting as a dream is actually a memory of something you saw that has haunted your subconscious," Emmy suggested. "That might explain why it felt so vivid."

He scratched his beard thoughtfully. "I don't know. I did a lot of guard work when I was a trooper, but I seldom paid attention to what we were guarding."

Her pulse pounded as she contemplated how to bring up her own work with Syndicorp. She had told no one except her best friend, Marlis, about the horrible experiments—not that the human gunslinger, with her short-term memory issues, remembered the confession. Swallowing thickly, Emmy said, "For a short while, I worked on a project using chambers like you describe. It was near one of the prison planets."

Eyes narrowing, Chigs said, "Which planet?"

Relieved he hadn't asked for specifics about her work, Emmy said, "Nunum-qa, but I'm sure the lab has been moved since I was there. Syndicorp is always one step ahead when it comes to ensuring their activities remain a secret from the general public."

"Still..." Chigs stood up, determination etched across his face. "We know Dollard's minions escaped with some of the denaidan prisoners in the lab we raided. Providing specifics might help Kashatok's contacts in the Cartel locate the lab's new location. We have to find those women before it's too late."

Emmy hesitated. It was highly unlikely Kashatok could locate the lab based on one man's dream and her own distant recollections, but between her guilt and the fire in Chigs's eyes, she was willing to try.

"All right," she agreed. "Let's go talk to Kashatok."

Chigs reached down to take her hand, his callouses rough against her palm. "I have faith in Ellam Cua's plan." He pulled her to her feet. "And in you, Emmy. We will find my mate together."

Emmy's heart skipped a beat as she looked into Chigs's eyes, the intensity of his faith radiating off him like a tangible force. In that moment, even she was tempted to believe his dream might be divine intervention. *Perhaps I can finally atone for my sins.*

Chapter Three

The scent of recycled oxygen mixed with the sharp tang of synthetic protein hit Chigs the moment he stepped into the ship's broad mess hall. He wrinkled his nose, noticing Emmy's pert nose do the same before she covered it with a pale, petite hand. One of the cyborgs must've been in charge of cooking again—they always seemed to burn the chow and end up having to use the replicators. But food was the last thing on Chigs's mind. He glanced at the crew members seated at the long tables near the galley doors, looking for Kasha-tok's bearded copper face.

At one end of the main table, Tovik spoke with animated exaggeration, eliciting a burst of harsh laughter from a handful of crew members. At the other end, Qaiyaan sat with his shaggy dark head close to Lisa, his human mate, lost in their own private world.

Emmy nudged Chigs's arm and pointed toward a long table to the right where Kashatok sat alone. His furry lavender netorpok, Jhikik, sat perched on his shoulder. The creature's eyes were half-lidded, as if sleepy, but the tip of its prehensile tail twitched with alertness. The little pest was probably just waiting for a chance to cause trouble.

Chigs strode over and slid onto the bench across from Kashatok, who had one hand wrapped around a bottle of Kantarellian rum. A platter of synthesized protein lumps in green gravy sat mostly untouched in front of him. Jhikik bared his tiny teeth as Kashatok pushed the bottle toward the newcomers. "Might want to drink your rations and avoid the food tonight."

"Thanks, *iluq*." Chigs accepted the rum and took a long pull directly from the bottle before offering it to Emmy. The small human tipped it back to drink without hesitation. He watched her slender throat ripple as she swallowed, appreciating a woman who wasn't afraid of a drink or two. It strengthened his belief that she was the right person to help with his mission.

A sudden cough set Emmy's brown curls bouncing, and she set the bottle down with a thud. Chigs reached over to thump her back, but Jhikik leaped to the table, then to Emmy's lap, chittering a warning. Chigs scowled and withdrew his hand. Those needle-sharp teeth had bitten him enough times to make Chigs wary of the little *tunrak.*

Emmy cleared her throat and stroked the beast's soft fur. "Aw, aren't you the cutest?"

Her smile made Chigs's secondary heart do a strange little double beat that he found unsettling. Reassured the creature wasn't hostile toward Emmy, Chigs returned to the task at hand. "Kashatok, I need your help organizing a mission."

Kashatok frowned. "What mission?"

"To find my mate." Chigs quickly explained his vision, pausing only briefly when Joy plopped down on the bench next to Kashatok. She was still in her work coveralls, a smudge of gray hydraulic fluid marring the tan skin on the side of her neck. She set a platter of green glop onto the table in front of her.

Kashatok put his arm around her, pulling her close while his other hand reached for the rum. "Don't eat that," he murmured into her short, dark hair.

Chigs felt a twinge of jealousy over the mated pair's obvious bond, but reminded himself that his mission would soon win him a mate of his own. He wrapped up his summary with, "We think the Cartel might have additional intel about the location of the lab."

Kashatok shook his head slowly. "You want me to contract with the Cartel over a dream?" He took a swig of rum. "I know we're between missions at the moment, Chigs, but that's a pretty big risk for something so uncertain. Hard data, maybe. But a dream?"

Emmy added, "It is a risk, but it's possible that it's based on a subconscious memory that could hold clues about Syndicorp activities. I've worked with chambers like he describes. They were on a base near Nunum-qa."

"It's not a dream. Ellam Cua sent me a vision." Chigs's chest puffed with certainty. "It led me to Emmy, and she—"

Tovik slid onto the bench near Chigs, gazing past him toward Emmy with a wistful expression. "Did I hear you say you and Emmy are mates? Congratulations."

Chigs realized more of the crew were now listening from the other table, likely jumping to similar conclusions. *Uminaq.* Better clear this up quickly. "Emmy's not my mate, kid, so you still have a chance."

Emmy stiffened, then shoved Chigs's shoulder. "Tovik and I have already had that discussion, Chigs. We're not compatible." Then she smiled at Tovik to soften the rejection. "But I'm proud to be his friend."

Kashatok pushed the rum toward the kid in silent sympathy, and Tovik gave him a stiff smile before taking a long a drink.

Feeling bad about putting both Emmy and Tovik on the spot, Chigs continued, "I can feel my mate calling me through our divine bond. She's in one of the pods Dollard's people took with them when they fled."

Tovik lowered the bottle, ginger eyebrows pinched with confusion. "So you haven't met her yet? I thought you needed physical contact to form the bond."

"Ellam Cua blessed me with a vision. I know this feeling is true." Chigs returned his focus to Kashatok. "Right now, I need Kashatok to contact the Cartel and see if they know anything about the lab in my vision."

Kashatok crossed his arms over his long beard. "I don't want to doubt you—or Ellam Cua, for that matter—but I'm not sure this would be the best use of our resources. Asking for help from the Cartel is expensive." He shifted his attention to the crew watching from the other table. "What do you think, Qaiyaan? Doug?"

Emmy interrupted. "Can't Doug just hack us the funds, as usual?" She glanced toward the cyborg male at the far end of the table. "I think we should at least ask them."

Warmth spread through Chigs at her support.

"How does the Cartel fit into all this?" Marlis asked from behind them. Chigs looked over his shoulder to where the gunslinger stood, hands on her hips over her gun belt. "I thought they were our enemies, too."

Lisa chimed in from the other table, her voice tinged with bitterness. "They are. The Cartel is just as ruthless and untrustworthy as Syndicorp, forcing colonies to pay protection money, running slaves, murdering entire families to keep their secrets. We'd do well to remember that."

Noatak rose and pulled Marlis over to sit on the bench next to Emmy. "The relationship between the Cartel and the rebellion is... complicated. Sometimes our interests align. Other times, they don't." He leaned in to address Kashatok. "But we can't always afford to be picky about our allies. If this is a lead, we should follow it."

The mess hall doors slid open to admit Mek and Rashana. Seeing the group clustered around the table, they hurried over, Rashana waddling in the late stages of pregnancy. "Sorry we're late," said Mek, shaking his head when Kashatok offered the rum. "We got caught up in the med bay."

"We're having a girl!" Rashana said, stroking a palm over the curve of her rounded belly. Her red gold face positively glowed with excitement, and everyone broke into congratulations. She was a human-denaidan hybrid, and her child would be the first born to the rebels in nearly two decades—and hopefully it wouldn't be the last.

The sight of her served as a stark reminder to Chigs that more than just finding his mate was on the line. The fate of the denaidan people hung in the balance.

Taking up where Noatak had left off, Chigs said, "So it's agreed. Kashatok will contact the Cartel."

Tovik's fingertips drummed a quick rhythm on the tabletop. "Instead of contacting the Cartel directly, why doesn't Doug hack into the darkweb? Seems like a safer bet."

All eyes turned expectantly to the cyborg, who was also the most powerful cyber-sensitive in existence. "I'm already looking," Doug said, his green cybernetic eye flashing as he sifted through data. Chigs marveled at the ease with which he could hack a computer system anywhere in the galaxy. "Is there a name for these chambers?"

"Yes," said Emmy. "Synaptic alteration chambers—SAC units for short. Syndicorp used them to experiment on prisoners."

The room fell silent until Doug spoke again. "I have located historical data about two labs using SAC units.

One on Nunam-qa and another on a moon orbiting Xeranis. The projects were defunded almost a cycle ago. The labs have reportedly been dismantled. I have also identified the director of the lab on Xeranis, a man named Dr. Dafari. He is now living on Aleigh."

"Dafari?" Emmy gasped.

Chigs turned to her. "You know him?"

"You could say that." There was a tightness to her eyes Chigs couldn't interpret, and a flush to her cheeks. Some denaidans could use their ionic power to sense heartbeat and temperature, to gauge a person's emotions, but Chigs had never had that sort of finesse. He was better at brute force.

Emmy cleared her throat before continuing, "He... he was my fiancé." She reached for the bottle of rum and took a long swig. "I can't believe he ended up being the director for that project. But then, he did move up the ranks faster than anybody I know."

Chigs's hearts skipped a rapid beat. *Emmy has an old flame in Syndicorp?* The thought made him uncomfortable, but it also made ever more sense why his dream sent him to her. "Any chance you could contact him? Find out what he knows?"

Emmy chewed her lower lip, doubt written all over her pale round face. "It would be strange for me to contact him out of the blue. We didn't part on the best of terms. And if he retired on Aleigh, he's in the heart of Syndicorp territory."

Disappointment settled like weights on Chigs's shoulders. Another dead end. And every passing moment increased the odds that his mate would be lost to him forever. Emmy's brown eyes were pinched in obvious distress, and he had a moment of empathy for her. Had she believed Dafari was her mate?

"I know!" Tovik exclaimed. "Mek and I can go undercover as Syndicorp doctors and lure this Dafari guy away so we can force him to reveal the lab's location. We'll tell him we have a confidential project we want him to oversee. All we need are lab coats and some fake credentials." He straightened his shoulders. "You can call me Dr. Vortex."

Laughter erupted around the table. "Tovik, I admire your imagination," Qaiyaan said, "but even if we put you in a lab coat, you wouldn't pass for a doctor. You're denaidan. There are no denaidans on Aleigh."

Mek chuckled. "Especially with a name like Dr. Vortex."

"Fine, figure it out yourself, then," said Tovik, crossing his arms. "I just thought you might want backup."

Mek was shaking his head. "Regardless of what you come up with, I can't help this time. I'm sorry. The baby could arrive any day now, and I'm the only medical doctor in the fleet."

"If anyone is going, it should be me," Chigs said. "I'll disguise myself with a hood or something."

Kashatok snorted. "In a hood? Plus, you know nothing about medicine. You really think you could pass for a doctor?"

Chigs scowled, filled with his own doubt. "This is the only plan we have, and I'll do whatever I have to find my mate."

Emmy interrupted, "Dafari's too smart to be duped into falling for a plan like that, even if we sent someone who could pass for a doctor." She set the bottle down with a plunk and lifted her chin defiantly. "I'll go. He and I lived together on Aleigh, so I have the best shot at finding him and getting the information we need."

Gratitude flooded through Chigs. It was obvious she didn't want to see the man again, yet she was putting herself in his path for the sake of this mission. He settled a hand on her shoulder, thinking how fragile her bones felt under his palm as he gently squeezed. "Thank you, Emmy."

She shrugged. "I'm just glad I can do my part in the rebellion."

Chigs's chest tightened as he realized he knew nothing about this Dafari fellow. Emmy could be heading into danger. He squeezed her shoulder gently. "I'll come as your bodyguard."

Emmy shook her head. "No. It would be strange if I showed up with an armed guard. Plus, we're back to the fact that there aren't any denaidans on Aleigh."

"But you can't go alone," he insisted. "I would never forgive myself if you were harmed. Let me pose as your bodyguard. I'll put on full battle gear and cover my head with a helmet."

"Dafari'd never buy it," she said.

"What if I craft a disguise for you?" the cyborg named Emilryde spoke softly from the other table. "I escaped the sex slave pens on Enays by disguising myself as a human. Cover your skin with makeup, shave your beard, and—"

"I'm not shaving my beard," Chigs said firmly. It'd taken him years to get his beard exactly how he liked it. "Humans have beards."

Emilryde grimaced. "Not like you denaidans."

"You don't need to shave," said Joy. "I did a bit of under-cover work for RealTime News. If we cover you in holo-reflective paint, we can use a portable projector to change your face and hide the beard."

"Okay," Chigs said. "That sounds reasonable."

"Assirpaa!" said Tovik. "I want in on the fun."

Emilryde rose from the bench. "It's settled, then. I'll start working on the holo-paint."

Chigs took another gulp of rum. He wasn't so sure about the fun part, but at least he got to keep his beard.

CHAPTER FOUR

Emmy's boots clicked against the polished metal floor, a rapid staccato to the slower thud of Chigs's stride. His dark braids swung with each impassioned gesture as he spoke about their upcoming plans, but she was barely listening.

They'd just left the mess hall, and the lingering buzz from the rum still warmed her blood. Discovering her ex had been promoted to head of the SAC program had been like a blow to the head. *But of course he was.* She recalled the look of disdain on his face when she'd questioned the ethics of their testing. Dafari wasn't one to let ethics hold him back from a promotion.

Dredging up her past with Dafari had been painful, but she also couldn't get the image of Mek's big hand tenderly pressed against Rashana's rounded stomach out of her mind—his kind eyes, his warm laugh. Why did she always seem to choose unavailable men? The ache in her heart pulsed.

Stupid girl. Seeing Mek with his new love, she'd wanted nothing more than to escape. She'd volunteered for the mission before her addled brain had time to realize she was only swapping one painful torment for a greater agony. Mek had been an unrequited dream. Dafari had almost been her forever…

And now she was on the hook to actually meet him again—hoping to wheedle out the very top-secret information that had caused their breakup.

What is wrong with me? It had to be the rum. It was the only reason she could think of for volunteering for this hare-brained mission. That, and Chigs's determination to move forward with a plan that would only get him killed.

"Emmy?" Chigs's voice pulled her back to the present. His deep-set eyes narrowed with concern. "Are you all right? You seem… distracted."

"I'm fine," she lied, touched by his concern. "Just anxious about the mission."

Chigs studied her face. "I was asking if you could tell me more about Dafari?"

"Oh." Emmy's chest tightened. *Talking about your feelings is the only way to let them go.* At least he wasn't asking her about her work on the project. Letting out a breath, she nodded. "Of course."

"What is his background?" Chigs asked as they turned a corner toward the living section.

"Dafari's parents are high-ranking officials for Syndicorp, and some people say he moved up the ranks so quickly because of their influence. But in all honesty, he's a brilliant neuroscientist." She couldn't keep the bitterness from her voice. "He's also obsessed with success—money, status, prestige."

"Are your parents also officials for the corp?"

She shook her head. "No. My dad's a professor at a small university and my mom's a nurse. They live in a colony on Candigas. But when Syndicorp recruited me, they were thrilled."

"Did they like Dafari?"

Emmy had only taken Dafari home to meet them once. Her parents had been gracious, but she'd felt a tangible strain in the air—like neither of them had quite been sure what to make of the high-ranking doctor or his lofty ambitions. Just before Emmy and Dafari were to return to Aleigh, her mother pulled her aside and told her not to let material things cloud her judgement when it came to relationships. And that was exactly Dafari— material.

"They were cordial," Emmy said. "But I don't think they liked him."

"But you loved him?"

She turned her gaze away, feeling a little embarrassed as she remembered how quickly she'd fallen for his wit and humor. "He's very charming."

"So what happened between you two?" Chigs asked, his voice softening.

"He's the one who got me the position on the SAC project. When I discovered what they were doing, I tried to talk him into quitting with me, into standing up for our ethics. He insisted Syndicorp was doing it for the greater good. Then he broke our engagement." Her throat felt tight as she continued, recalling the cold look on his face as he broke the news. "He said that if I didn't believe in the project, we couldn't be together. I was a distraction, and he needed to stay focused on his work."

Chigs made a small angry sound but didn't interrupt.

"I packed up my things and left that night." Flashes of the apartment they'd shared rolled through her mind. The white and gold his and hers towels. The silky comforter she'd bought for the bed. The abstract painting he'd given her for her birthday that she'd never quite liked but never admitted. "The next day, before I could even show up for work and turn in my resignation, I received notice of my termination from the project and a reminder about my non-disclosure agreement." She stared at the deck as they walked, not wanting Chigs to see the tears filming her eyes. "I got a couple of job offers in other departments after that, but I didn't want to work for Syndicorp anymore."

As they passed the wide doorway to the observation deck, she felt the press of warm fingers around hers. Chigs squeezed gently until she stopped waling and looked up into his kind eyes. "We are happy you joined us, Emmy. I admire your bravery."

She squeezed back, comforted, before pulling free and looking through the doorway at the star-studded expanse on the other side of the doorway. "Thank you. I just wish I'd been able to stop the experiments."

"We all have our share of guilt." His voice was laden with regret. "When I was a trooper for Syndicorp, I followed orders without question. I trusted our leaders to do the right thing. It's even possible I was near denaidan females, maybe even my future mate, without ever being aware of it."

"You couldn't have known. It's not your fault."

He sighed. "Perhaps not. But I still carry the guilt. I'll do whatever it takes to find my mate and the other denaidan females. And I'm grateful to have you by my side."

Emmy straightened her spine. She envied the denaidans' certainty that a perfect mate awaited him. Her own romantic hopes had crumbled to dust too many times to have that kind of faith, but at least she might help Chigs with his. "I'm happy I can help."

Turning away from the view of the stars, they continued down the hall toward the crew quarters until they reached a fork in the passageway. "I'm this way," she said.

Chigs pointed the other direction. "I'm that way." He turned to face her, his expression earnest. "Emmy, thank you again for believing in my vision. It means...more than I can express."

Emmy felt a pang of longing deep in her chest, an ache for something she knew she would never have—a mate like Chigs. He was not only sexy, as were all denaidans, he was strong, loyal, and brave—everything anyone could want in a partner. At least this time, she knew up front he was already dedicated to another.

"I'm happy to help, Chigs," she replied, trying to keep her voice steady. "But this is for more than just you and your future mate. The entire rebellion wants to save those women, me included."

With a nod, Chigs turned down the branch leading to his quarters, leaving Emmy standing alone in the hallway. She headed toward her room, each step feeling heavier than the last. She dreaded seeing Dafari again—if she could even arrange a meeting. He'd been very decisive when he broke things off. What if he refused to even speak to her?

Embarrassment heated her cheeks even thinking about the possibility. Not only were Chigs's hopes riding on her ability to pull this off, but the crew was putting forth a lot of effort to make it happen. Positive thoughts, Emmy. She forced herself to imagine the opposite, where Dafari welcomed her back with open arms, told her he regretted everything he'd said, and wanted to join the rebels to bring Syndicorp to its knees.

Snorting at the impossible dream, she paused in front of her door and stared at the mural of vibrant flowers painted on the surface. It was meant to be cheerful, but the garish colors all seemed to clash. With a sigh, Emmy turned away, knowing she was too anxious to fall asleep.

"Chronic low-grade depression," Emmy muttered under her breath, diagnosing herself with practiced ease. She knew better than anyone that bottling up emotions could lead to disaster, and a conversation with a friend might do her some good.

She turned back the way she'd come, taking the lift to the deck with the firing range. Marlis would most likely be there, and a conversation with a friend would do Emmy some good.

The firing range doors slid open to the sharp crackle of a pulse weapon's discharge, and she spotted Marlis's platinum blond head across the room, standing at the ready line, her feet braced wide and a long rifle butted up against her shoulder. A metallic tang wafted out from recently fired bolts, while holographic targets darted and weaved across the far wall, challenging even the most skilled marksmen.

"Mind if I join you?" Emmy called out.

Marlis lowered the rifle and looked over her shoulder with a wide smile. "Hey! What are you doing here? Looking for a lesson on shooting before your mission?"

"Sure," Emmy replied, moving forward to accept the spare pistol Marlis offered. Perhaps a little target practice would make her feel less helpless.

Marlis reminded her of the basics—how to hold a weapon, how to line up a shot—then pointed toward a target shaped like the silhouette of a human male. "Now just imagine that's your scumbag ex and squeeze the trigger."

Sighting in on the target, Emmy fired eight shots in rapid succession, missing every time. Her arm slumped to her side. "Fuuuuck."

"Aww, shit," Maris said, taking the pistol and setting it aside before pulling Emmy into a hug. "You're all worked up. What's the matter?"

"I always fall for the wrong guy," Emmy said through gritted teeth. "First Dafari, then Mek. Nobody wants me. I guess I need to just accept that I'm meant to be alone."

"Emmy, you're a catch." Marlis patted her back. "You'll find someone when the time is right. Stop dwelling on the past and focus on the future."

"You mean the future where I go confront my ex?" Emmy scowled and pulled away. "I can't believe I actually volunteered for this."

Marlis grimaced. "Look at it as your chance to make him regret the day he left you." She smoothed her fingertips along the barrel of her rifle. "And Chigs is pretty easy on the eyes. If I wasn't already mated to Noatak…"

"Marlis!" Emmy exclaimed. "The point of the mission is to rescue his mate and other denaidan females. Remember?"

"Right, right," Marlis muttered, looking sheepish. "I forgot. But still, he's not mated yet, and anything can happen when two people face danger together."

Emmy blew out a resigned breath. "He's clearly and completely dedicated to someone else." She picked up the pistol, relishing its solid heft against her palm. "Plus, I've decided I'm not falling in love ever again. Especially not with a denaidan—if this mission is successful, they'll have females of their own species they'll want to bond with."

"Never say never, Emmy. Nobody knows what the future holds." Marlis reached out and disengaged the safety on Emmy's pistol before pointing toward the target on the far wall. "Just take everything one shot at a time, okay?"

Emmy nodded. Marlis was right. The only way to move forward with anything was one step at a time. She steadied her hand and squeezed the trigger, obliterating the target in a shower of sparks. A meager sense of accomplishment washed through her. *One shot at a time.* She only hoped she had enough ammo.

Chapter Five

Chigs tried not to wrinkle his nose as the tacky holo-reflective paint on his face, beard, and hair finished drying. The stuff smelled metallic and made his beard itch, but was better than the lingering scent of sweat and stale cologne in the onboard locker room. "Why do I need the paint again?"

"The projector needs a reflective surface to work properly," Joy said. She was helping Emmy paw through the contents of several abandoned lockers, looking for human clothing for his disguise. They would've programmed some clothes, but Tovik had recently attempted to upgrade the *Icarus's* fashion replicators and accidentally knocked the system offline.

"This pigment will match the skin color programmed for your face," said Emilryde as he rubbed a brown paste over Chigs's hands. "Like the holo-paint, should stay on for almost a week. You'll need to use a solvent to remove it completely."

"Thanks." Chigs knew little about Emilryde except that he was an enayshuan, most likely royalty given the dust tattoos gleaming across his dark skin. At least the guy seemed confident in his disguise work. Chigs wondered how he'd ended up in the slave pens on Enays, but didn't want to pry. "Are you sure my beard and hair aren't a problem?"

Joy came over and looped a chain with a small silver pendant around Chigs's throat. "Why don't we try it out?"

A faint shimmering field enveloped Chigs, and he heard Emmy gasp. When he looked in the mirror, his dark beard and long braids had vanished, replaced by short-cropped sandy brown hair and a clean-shaven jawline. Chigs turned his head from side to side, fingers going to his beard—his reflection stroked the empty space below his chin. If he didn't know better, he'd think he was staring into the face of a human stranger.

Joy whistled in satisfaction. "Wow. Tovik outdid himself. As long as Chigs stays out of trouble, he'll blend right in."

"Just keep your hands off the beard," Emilryde added. "Or people might wonder what's up."

"Also, the projector's charge only lasts a couple of days," Joy said. "You'll need to charge it periodically."

He nodded and dropped his hand. Remembering not to touch his beard was going to be difficult.

Emmy stepped forward, eyes full of approval, and held up a pair of dark slacks and a yellow shirt made of loose, lightweight fabric. "These should fit. All you need now is a convincing backstory to go along with your disguise."

"How about posing as newlyweds on a romantic getaway?" Twerp piped up from where she'd been quietly observing, her robotic voice full of enthusiasm.

Chigs rolled his eyes. "That's the worst cover story I've ever heard."

Emmy tapped her chin thoughtfully, a wicked gleam filling her eyes. "Not really. Dafari might believe I came back to show off my new man. Especially one as big as you are."

"Ha! Yes!" Joy chortled. "Boy, do I miss undercover work." She eyed Chigs again. "But you didn't start life as a newlywed. You need more history."

He'd been thinking about that all night, worried about his storytelling abilities. "My parents were farmers on Denaida-daru, so I know a bit about that. What if I come from an agricultural colony?"

"How about Jarboa?" offered Joy. "It's small and outside Syndicorp space."

"Jarboa. Got it." Chigs nodded.

"That's a great idea," Emmy said. "Dafari has no interest in outback colonies or agriculture."

Happy she approved, he continued. "I left home to join the troopers and became a decorated officer. I once led a daring rescue mission to save hostages from an outlaw group."

Joy raised a skeptical eyebrow. "Maybe we should leave out any association with the troopers."

"I think it's okay," Emmy said. "Dafari was never one to pay attention to military operations, so I don't think he'll ask questions. And it's a good explanation of how Chigs ended up leaving the colony." She winked at him. "Plus, he knows I've always had a thing for soldiers. We'll say we met right after you ended your tour of duty."

Even though he knew they were discussing a fictional past, there was something about the way she looked at him that made him feel like he really was a hero. He held onto that feeling, knowing it would help sell his disguise even more convincingly. He winked back. "And I for smart women."

She flushed and turned back to the lockers, muttering something about finding the right sized shoes.

"All right, then," Joy conceded with a grin. "Farmer-turned-hero it is. Just remember to keep that charm in check, Chigs, or you'll have girls hanging all over you."

He frowned, turning away from Emmy. "But I am supposed to be married."

Emmy and Joy both laughed. "To some women, that will make you even more attractive," said Emmy.

"You will also need a story about how you met and fell in love." Twerp sighed and clasped her metal appendages together in front of her. "Humans always ask couples questions like 'how did you meet?' and 'when did you know they were the one?' Oh!" She rocked back and forth on her treads. "What if you were childhood sweethearts torn apart by feuding families, only to reunite years later?"

"That won't fit the cover story, Twerp," Emmy pointed out. "Dafari knows I grew up on Candigas, and we're saying Chigs grew up farming on Jarboa."

"Oh." Twerp's mechanical arms fell to her sides with a double clank.

"We met at a space station bar," Chigs said firmly. "One glance across the crowded room and—bam!—I knew she was the one for me."

Emmy smiled sadly. "I suppose I did frequent quite a few seedy saloons after Dafari and I ended things."

A flare of protectiveness rose in Chigs's chest at the thought of Emmy drowning her sorrows at a bar, especially sorrows over some idiot who let her go.

"What about cute nicknames for each other?" Twerp asked hopefully. "Humans in love are always using pet names."

Chigs immediately knew what he wanted to call Emmy. "How about *piayagaq*? It means 'little finger.' My father used to call my mother that because she had him wrapped around hers."

"That's sweet," Emmy said, one hand over her heart.

"Yeah, but it's also a mouthful." Joy laughed. "Maybe he should use something a little more human? Sweetheart or honey would be good."

Face heating, Chigs nodded. He was supposed to be disguised as a human, after all, and his affection for

Emmy wouldn't be real.

Emmy blinked up at him, an odd expression on her face. "What about peanut? It sounds sort of like pia... pia... what you said."

"Peanut," Chigs repeated before breaking into a grin. "I like it."

The sound of the door opening drew their attention, and Attie, Doug's mate, entered, smiling brightly. She paused and surveyed Chigs with raised blond brows. "Wow. Is that you, Chigs?" When he nodded, she continued. "Well done. Doug forged an identification chip for you. You're now Charles Montague. And he booked a reservation in the honeymoon suite at the Starlight Resort on Aleigh."

"Honeymoon suite?" Chigs asked, gaping. Their cover needed to look authentic, but he hadn't thought about them spending time alone in a room together.

Emmy looked as uncomfortable as he felt. "Makes sense since we're posing as newlyweds." She began nervously picking up discarded clothing and stuffing it back into lockers. "And nobody will know what we do—uh, don't do—in the privacy of our own suite."

"Honeymoon." Emilryde crossed his arms and scoffed. "How strange to put so much value on the sexual act that you make a whole ritual out of it."

"It's not about sex as much as it is about intimacy," Emmy said, her face now bright pink.

"And humans aren't the only species with an isolation ritual for new couples," Chigs added, feeling an instinctive need to defend Emmy's culture.

"Fair point," Emilryde conceded.

Kashatok poked his head into the room. "We'll be at the drop point soon," he announced. His eyes widened as they fell on Chigs. "*Assirpaa!* Chigs?"

Chigs grinned, standing taller as he looked in the mirror at the reflection of his human-looking self. "Call me Charles."

With an appreciative whistle, Kashatok gestured toward the hallway behind him. "The shuttle's ready whenever you are. Should only take you a few hours to reach Whylon Station."

"I'm ready." Chigs glanced toward Emmy. "You?"

She nodded. "I just need to grab my bag from my room."

As they moved to leave, Emilryde called out, "Have fun on your honeymoon!"

"Very funny," Chigs muttered, rolling his eyes. But he had an odd feeling this mission was going to test his restraint in ways he hadn't anticipated.

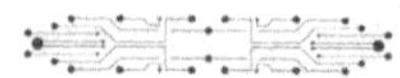

Chigs piloted the shuttle away from the *Icarus* toward the pinprick of light that was Whylon space station. From there, they'd catch a commercial transport to Aleigh, solidifying their cover as newlyweds on honeymoon.

In the co-pilot seat beside him, Emmy studied her datapad intently, listing off facts about Jarboa they should both know by heart. They'd decided that their fictional life together would be on his home planet once they'd finished their honeymoon, but that Chigs—now Charles—hadn't been back there in many cycles, which gave them an out if there were any discrepancies in their story.

"If we run into anyone I know on Aleigh, we need to look comfortable and natural with each other, like we've been together for a while. We, um…" Emmy scrunched up her nose in that way she had, which he found disturbingly charming. "We're going to have to hold hands a lot."

"Easy enough." He reached over and gently clasped her small hand in his large one. Her skin was soft, and a jolt of electricity raced through him as her fingers entwined with his. Chigs's hearts raced at the sensation, and he wondered if Emmy felt it too. "No one can tear us apart now. We're going to see the galaxy together, just the two of us."

Emmy smirked. "Joy's right about you being a charmer."

He grinned back, liking the compliment, and gave her hand a squeeze. "Only for you, peanut."

Her smirk transformed into a wistful smile, and she gently pulled her hand free to lean forward and look out the view screen. "There's the station."

He wanted to ask her what made her look sad, but was forced to focus on piloting the shuttle as the multi-colored lights of Whylon Station resolved into a fortress of spires and turrets. The station had been continuously added to and remodeled over the centuries, resulting in a veritable maze—both inside and out. He'd only been on the station once in passing, but he'd studied the docking schematics so that he could easily find the secure landing slip Doug had arranged for them.

He maneuvered through traffic and threaded his way between the spires, keeping an eye out for any Syndicorp ships. The Cartel controlled Whylon, but the station was technically inside Syndicorp space, and was often used as neutral ground for dealings between both entities.

He maneuvered the shuttle into place and engaged the docking clamps. Rising from his seat, he shouldered their bags, missing the weight of a pulse pistol on his hip. Emmy had insisted a weapon would draw attention worn out in the open, so he'd packed the gun, but he'd kept a combat knife stashed in his boot. Whylon Station could be a dangerous place.

As the airlock cycled open, Emmy looped one arm through his, her voice barely audible above the hiss of stabilizing air pressure. "Ready for showtime?"

"Ready," Chigs agreed, squeezing her arm against his side.

Together, they stepped out into the bustling spaceport. Various species of travelers from across the galaxy hurried along the corridors, striding, slithering, or floating in hover carts. Most were traders, but a few tourists used the station as a jump point for more remote regions of the galaxy. The residents on Whylon trended toward seedy, and Chigs wrapped a protective arm around Emmy's shoulders, pulling her close as they dodged a pair of long-clawed rakwiji stalking through the crowd. He felt the hairs on the back of his neck rise as the scaled beings drew closer and had a moment of worry that his disguise had been compromised until one of them grabbed a frail-looking finofan by the shoulder and shoved him against the wall.

Shouting erupted behind them as Chigs urged Emmy along. They passed several shop keepers hawking their wares, and Emmy's steps faltered when she caught sight of a mannequin in a brilliant red dress. "Oh, wow. That's gorgeous."

"I'll buy you something pretty when we reach Aleigh," he said, loud enough for people around to hear as he pulled her away.

She seemed to shake herself back into reality, her pace increasing to match his until they were forced to pause and wait for a long line of six-legged yanipa-nimayu carrying heavy loads on their backs to cross the corridor. The surrounding crowd grumbled at the delay, but Emmy leaned into him and smiled sweetly, looking into his eyes. The top of her curly head barely reached his collarbone, and he gratefully inhaled her sweet fragrance above the pungent scent of foreign spices and alien bodies filling the station. She was doing a damn good job playing the part of a new bride, and he had to remind himself her affection was an act. Though, to be fair, he was equally surprised about how easy he found it to play the part of a smitten groom; his hearts were racing like he really was in love.

The last of the yanipa-nimayu passed by, and Emmy stiffened as a voice called out. "Emmy?"

Chapter Six

Emmy's pulse kicked up a notch at the sight of a slender human woman with dark hair and penetrating gray eyes elbowing past a family of bright blue finofan.

"Emmy Voss!" The woman came to an abrupt halt before them. "I can't believe it's you!"

"Hi Laurna." Emmy forced a smile. She'd met Laurna a few years back at a psychology seminar. Emmy had been wrapping up her medical credits to earn her next promotion, but Laurna had been more interested in collecting gossip about their colleagues.

Laurna yanked Emmy into a hug, which Emmy returned, though they hadn't been close. Stepping back, Laurna swept her gaze over Chigs. "And who's this tall drink of water?"

The appreciative glint in Laurna's eyes made Emmy's blood heat with possessiveness. Sure, Chigs wasn't really her husband, but Laurna didn't know that. Putting her arm around Chigs's waist, Emmy said, "This is my husband, Charles. We're heading to Aleigh for our honeymoon." She leaned her cheek against his broad chest and gave Laurna a look that made it very clear Chigs was off limits. "Charles, this is Laurna. We met at a seminar back in my Syndicorp days."

Chigs nodded politely, but Emmy could feel the tension in his frame. "Pleasure, Laurna," he said.

Laurna's gray eyes flickered with curiosity. "I'll be. Everyone wondered where you'd gone off to after, well..." The woman leaned closer to whisper loudly, "Dafari told me what happened. Losing your job like that must've been devastating. I think I'd have overreacted, too."

Emmy frowned, questions filling her mind too quickly to track. What had Dafari been telling people?

With a smile that showed every one of her very white teeth, Laurna continued. "But look at you now! Happily married. We simply must get together for lunch so we can catch up."

Chigs tightened his arm around her waist. "Peanut, we're going to miss our flight if we don't hurry."

"Of course," Emmy responded, her voice higher-pitched than usual. "It was great seeing you, Laurna. I'll look you up after the honeymoon. Travel safely."

"You too, you adorable lovebirds!"

Once they were out of sight, Chigs slowed his stride and whispered, "Is she going to cause us trouble?"

"I don't think so. But I expect word about my new husband may reach Dafari before we do."

"At least it reinforces our story."

"Yes, but now we need a cover for why we were on Whylon Station. It's in the opposite direction of Jarboa from Aleigh." She flinched as a nearby g'naxian bellowed something at a companion, who laughed with equal gusto.

Chigs stepped around to put himself between her and them, guiding her onward with one hand at the small of her back. "We've been exploring the galaxy, remember? We're on our way back from a tour of the magnificent waterfalls on Pexa."

Emmy had only seen the exotic, mountainous planet in holos, but she'd always thought it would be an amazing place to visit. "Have you been to Pexa?"

He nodded. "Once, on a brief stop during my tour of duty. I didn't get to leave the Syndicorp outpost, and always swore I'd go back to see the falls. If my mate can travel, perhaps I'll take her there for a visit."

"I'm sure she'd love that," Emmy said, keeping the envy from her voice as she pretended to examine the pastry display in a nearby bake shop.

Chigs urged her along with a gentle tug. "Our ship's just ahead."

They pushed through the crowd until they reached the gangway and hurried on board. The vessel, once a small luxury cruise ship, had been converted to a transport shuttle, and the seats were worn but comfortable. Once they'd settled in, Chigs reclined and closed his eyes. Emmy watched the traffic through the nearby view screen as they pulled away from Whylon Station. Though she'd met plenty of other species in her life, she had traveled little, and the unfamiliar ships orbiting the station intrigued her. Some were sleek and smooth, while others looked clunky and downright awkward.

The trip to Aleigh went by in a blur, and soon the bright green and blue planet filled the viewscreen. Emmy watched the glittering spires of buildings covering most of the planet grow closer. Resorts spread along a sandy beach as far as the eye could see, and patches of lush green forest dotted the metropolis—designated sanctuaries for the planet's dwindling wildlife.

After the ship settled to the ground at the spaceport, Emmy and Chigs disembarked, making their way through the open-air concourse interspersed with palm trees swaying gently in the breeze. As they rode a private ground transport to the resort, Emmy surveyed the sleek buildings soaring high above them, reflecting sunlight from their crystalline polymer surfaces. An advertisement flashed across the surface of one building, a larger-than-life promise of younger skin. Another ad for all-in-one cleaning bots spewed from a holographic drone floating between the palms.

"Welcome to Aleigh," she muttered, voice barely audible over the hum of the transport's engine. "Quite a sight, isn't it?" She'd once loved everything about this planet and city, but now her stomach roiled at the sight of Syndicorp propaganda plastered on every available surface.

"Mm," Chigs agreed. "How long did you live here?"

"Four years," Emmy said, catching a glimpse of her favorite restaurant down a side street. It reminded her of Dafari, and she again wondered what he'd been telling people about their breakup and her subsequent disappearance.

The transport pulled up to the classically grand front entrance of the Starlight Resort, the crowning glory of Aleigh's capital city. The resort's central tower rose high above every building in the city, and its surrounding campus of gardens and activities stretched along the beach as far as the eye could see.

While a bellhop with graying hair and a pleasant smile carried their luggage, Emmy and Chigs strolled between the gilded columns lining the lobby. The air hummed with conversations and laughter as guests sipped iced beverages and listened to a pianist playing softly in one corner. Cut flowers in large vases were scattered about, filling the air with subtle perfume.

Emmy kept her attention on Chigs, finding it easy to feign adoration. His human disguise was flattering, and with his towering height, he garnered several discreet looks from passing women. She couldn't help the flush of pride at the jealousy in their eyes, though she honestly preferred his copper skin and full denaidan beard.

They reached the check-in desk where the concierge greeted them with a red-lipsticked smile. "Welcome to the Starlight Resort." She held out the pad of a biometric scanner. "Please sign in here."

Emmy reached forward and pressed her palm to the surface. The scanner chimed, and the concierge offered the pad to Chigs. Throat tight, Emmy watched him touch the pad. What if the scanner detected Chigs wasn't human? She didn't realize she was holding her breath until the concierge set the scanner aside.

"I see you've reserved our classic honeymoon suite, Mr. and Mrs. Montague." The concierge beamed at them and motioned for the bellhop. "Congratulations. Ronny will be happy to show you to your room."

They followed the bellhop to a transparent maglev elevator. Once inside, Chigs pulled her back against his chest and gazed out over the tall buildings glittering orange in the light of the setting sun. She could feel his heartbeat as she leaned against him, and for a moment, she simply allowed herself to get lost in the fantasy. So what if this wasn't real? She could imagine it was for now. "Isn't this amazing, honey?"

"Absolutely," Chigs agreed, leaning down to brush a feather-light kiss on her cheek. Though Emmy couldn't see his beard past his disguise, its tickle against her skin sent a delicious shiver down her spine.

They stepped off the elevator directly into the foyer of their suite, and Emmy drew in a sharp breath. Opalescent walls in soft pastel pink mimicked the tropical sunset outside, and plush furniture and fresh flowers decorated the space. A bank of floor-to-ceiling windows across the room opened onto a balcony overlooking the city, while seductive, ambient music played from invisible speakers.

"Allow me to show you some of our select amenities," said the bellhop, setting the bags to the side. "Our advanced AI systems can sense your body temperature, pheromones, and intoxication level. It will automatically adjust the suite's sound, colors, and scents according to your moods." He opened a small panel in the wall near the door, revealing a replication unit, and pressed the keypad. A tray with a bottle and two glass flutes materialized. "Please enjoy our gift of complimentary champagne and strawberries. The replicator is also programmed with a selection of cocktails and delectable meals from our top chefs."

Emmy eyed the replicator with excitement, wondering what foods she could make. The resort had always been well out of her price range, and she wondered if she'd have time to enjoy the amenities, considering the seriousness of her current mission.

The bellhop gestured toward the view of the city through the balcony doors. "The balcony is protected by a seamless energy shield for your safety and affords one-way viewing for complete privacy from the outside world." He then led the way through a set of double doors to where a massive bed sat on a platform in the center of the room. It was surrounded by gauzy, iridescent curtains and covered in a silken coverlet that reminded her of melted chocolate. He didn't pause, as if the room needed no explanation, passing quickly into the washroom.

The divine scent of flowers and musk washed over Emmy as she stepped into an enormous space styled with blue tiles that reminded her of the ocean. Shimmering water cascaded like a small waterfall into an extra-large tub with scented steam rising from its surface.

"The two-person jacuzzi tub is constantly refreshed with water sourced from the Starlight Resort's mineral spring and has several tactile enjoyment settings for your pleasure." The bellhop opened a discreet panel on the wall. "You can find a list of options here, as well as a replication unit for intimate toys and apparel."

Emmy swallowed thickly, suddenly imagining Chigs's naked, muscular body lounging in the tub's warmth. Chigs's hand tightened around hers, and she glanced over to find him staring back at her with an intensity that sent a flood of heat between her legs. The ambient melody in the suite shifted subtly to a provocative beat.

The bellhop cleared his throat, repressing an obvious smile. "We hope you will leave the Starlight Resort feeling like you've experienced your own personal paradise." With a slight bow, he departed, footsteps quickly fading as he left the suite.

Mortified, Emmy pulled her hand free of Chigs's, heart pounding hard against her ribs. *Get a hold of yourself, Emmy.* The damned AI controlling the suite's settings was definitely primed for newlyweds, reacting to her mere thought about Chigs's physique. She was going to have to practice some serious mental control.

"I… um… I need some air," Chigs said in a low voice. Then he spun and strode from the washroom.

Emmy closed her eyes and tried to think about fluffy kittens or scrubbing toilets—anything but sex. But she couldn't scrub images of Chigs' naked, wet body from her mind. Groaning, she splashed cold water on her face and scrubbed it with a towel. This stay was going to be more complicated than she'd imagined.

CHAPTER SEVEN

Chigs hurried away, trying to ignore the enormous bed as he strode toward the balcony and prayed fresh air would help clear his head. *You're on a quest to rescue your mate.* Yet all he could think about was getting Emmy naked and into the warm water of that jacuzzi tub. Of pressing his mouth to hers while he slicked soap along her luscious curves...

Uminaq! He needed to get a grip on himself before he did something rash. How could he even think about being with Emmy when his mate was out there, suffering at the hands of Syndicorp? And what might Emmy think of him if she suspected his thoughts? The suite's AI was going to make it hard to hide the direction of his thoughts if it kept ramping up the mood music.

The balcony doors slid open at his approach, revealing a cozy loveseat upholstered in sensual swirls and a small table with two padded chairs. Even the furniture seemed to beckon a couple to sit and stare into each other's eyes. Sheer curtains fluttered in the cool evening breeze, muting the city's sea of twinkling lights stretching out toward the horizon, while romantic music played in the background.

He shoved the curtains aside and stood at the railing, taking slow, deep breaths while his hearts continued to beat out a complex rhythm against his ribs. The air carried the scent of jasmine, reminding him of Emmy's delicate perfume. He groaned. Was there no escape from this torment? The pressure of his cock inside his slacks was growing painful, and the guilt roiling in his gut was making him nauseous.

Closing his eyes, he concentrated on his destined mate. *I'm going to rescue her.* But all he could see were Emmy's warm brown eyes and the way her smile made him feel lighter inside. The pretense of a relationship must be affecting his rational thought. That was it; he'd been so focused on finding his mate, even pretending that he was in love with Emmy was confusing him. He rolled his shoulders. The sooner he and Emmy contacted Dafari and ended this charade, the better.

Looking at his brown hands gripping the rail, he realized he was still disguised as a human. He should charge the holo projector to full capacity before the meeting with Dafari. He was about to lift the chain from around his neck and go in when he heard Emmy say from behind him. "Are you hungry? I programmed a meal for us."

She stood in the doorway holding a tray like a peace offering, her delicate features bathed in moonlight. His hearts constricted again. *It's only a meal with a fellow crew member,* he reminded himself. *Just think of her as one of your iluq.* "Sounds good," he said, forcing his attention to remain on her face instead of the curve of her breasts. "Just let me set this to charge."

He retrieved the charge unit from their luggage and put the projector in it, then returned to the balcony to find Emmy sitting at the small patio table. She lifted the lid from a covered dish on the tray she'd brought, releasing a savory smelling steam. "I wasn't certain what you liked, so I brought several options." The dish held chunks of meat in a golden sauce arranged on a bed of grain. Another dish held a roasted fowl and small, herbed tubers.

His stomach growled, and he realized he hadn't eaten since this morning. "It smells delicious." Taking the seat opposite her, he helped himself to the food. His first bite was salty with a hint of a kick, and before he knew it, he was reaching for seconds.

She held up her fork and examined a small piece of beige tuber on the end. "I wonder what it would cost us to get this programmed into the replicator on the *Icarus*. It's nice to be eating something besides kemeg stew."

He swallowed another bite of meat and licked his lips. "We'll have to ask Doug if he can download a copy."

"Mm-hm," she nodded, closing her eyes in obvious pleasure as she placed the bite in her mouth. The move was innocent enough, but the way her lips pursed around the fork got him thinking about other things her mouth might do. The music drifted into a sultry beat, and he clamped down on his thoughts. He didn't know how much more of this he could take.

Pushing away from the table, he twisted away from her, gazing out over the city lights. "Are you ready to contact Dafari?"

"Oh." Emmy's fork clinked against her plate and she cleared her throat, clearly uncomfortable. "I think it will look suspicious if we contact Dafari this soon after our arrival. We probably ought to spend a day or two holed up here—we're supposed to be on our honeymoon, after all."

Chigs stifled another groan. The longer they took, the more danger his mate could be in. But more importantly, what the hell were he and Emmy going to do to pass the time? His cock certainly had some ideas. *Stop thinking about that.* He forced himself to nod. "That makes sense."

A few moments of silence passed between them until Emmy said, "My father used to say that every person we meet has something new to teach us. I feel like we hardly know each other. Tell me something about yourself. Something few people know."

He considered her question. Nobody had ever asked him that before. He thought back to his childhood on Denaida-daru, before he'd joined Syndicorp or met any of his current *iluq*. "When I was younger, I used to enjoy carving small sculptures out of wood," he said. "I'd give them to the younger kids in the village to play with."

"Really?" Emmy smiled. "I never would've guessed. Do you still like to carve?"

"I haven't in a while." He reached down and drew his combat knife from his boot, recalling the feel of a blade biting into the grain of the wood. "Not many stray branches lying about on a spaceship. What about you? What did you enjoy doing as a kid?"

"Oh, I loved to dance." Her eyes lit with excitement. "Ballet, jazz, anything." The ambient music's beat kicked up a notch, as if in invitation, and Emmy tapped her fingers in time to the rhythm. "There's something so freeing about losing yourself in music and movement."

"I don't believe I've ever danced," Chigs admitted.

She gaped at him. "Never?"

He shook his head and noticed a worried look cross her face before she practically jumped up from her seat. "You need to learn how."

Chigs stared at her. "Now?"

"Yes. Now." She extended a hand to him. "Dafari will never believe our story if you don't. He knows how much I love it."

Swallowing a sudden knot in his throat, he reached up and accepted her grasp, allowing her to pull him to his feet.

"It's easy once you get the hang of it." Drawing him closer, she swayed her hips to the sultry beat. "Just let the music guide you."

Chigs found himself mesmerized by the graceful way she moved her body.

She stretched her arms up to place her hands on his shoulders. Her subtle perfume filled his senses, and her eyes sparkled as she craned her neck to smile up at him. "Damn, you're tall. This'll be interesting. Put your hands on my hips."

As if in a trance, he settled his palms against the curve of her waist.

She began swaying her hips in time to the music. "Now try to follow my lead."

Stepping left, then right, she showed him how to bring his body into sync with hers. Her hair brushed his arms like silken feathers, and her full breasts pressed against his lower ribs with distracting frequency. He stumbled, stepping on her toes. But when he tried to apologize, she merely laughed and insisted they keep going. *Uminaq*, he could listen to her laugh for hours.

Before long, they were twirling around the balcony. This was more fun than he'd expected, and Emmy felt so natural in his arms. As the song faded to a close, he picked her up around the waist and spun, eliciting another peal of laughter.

Emmy pulled away. "Wow, I'm thirsty!" Her voice shook slightly from exertion. "How about some champagne?"

Before he could answer, she disappeared inside, then returned with the bottle on a tray. She popped the cork and poured two fizzing glasses, handing him one. Raising her glass, she said, "To finding your mate."

The reminder was a sobering slug to the gut. He raised his glass in salute before emptying it in one swallow. It wasn't Kantarellian rum, but hopefully the champagne would be strong enough to dull the ache in his balls. "To finding my mate," he said.

Before I do something stupid.

Emmy's heart pounded from more than the dancing as she settled back into her chair on the balcony, glad for the small table between her and Chigs. His human disguise had created a barrier of sorts between them, but now that he'd turned off his holo projector, she wanted to run her hands over his beard and explore the hard planes of his gleaming copper skin. He was making her feel emotions she simply couldn't allow herself to feel, especially for him. *He's taken,* she reminded herself. *Devoted to another.*

She cleared her throat, uncomfortable with the tension filling the air. *Just steer the conversation to safe topics.* Her counseling job was mostly getting people to talk, after all. "So, do you have any siblings?" she asked. A pained look creased his face, and she immediately realized her mistake. His world had been destroyed, his family was likely dead. "I'm sorry. I wasn't thinking—"

"It's okay," he said. "I had a sister. She was a lot older than I was, and we weren't very close."

He went on to tell her about growing up on a farm, of long days spent in the fields tending crops and animals. "I used to stand in the fields near our house and stare up at the night sky for hours, imagining what it would be like to travel to all of them. My father thought I was crazy, but when a Syndicorp recruiter came along, I jumped at the chance to get off-world."

"That's why I joined, too," she said, pouring them both more champagne. "To get off world. My parents lived in dozens of colonies on many planets before I was born, but once I came along, they decided they were done with traveling. I always envied their adventures."

"What places have you visited?" he asked.

"Just two moons around Aleigh," she admitted, remembering the city perched on the edge of a mining crater where she'd done some temp work. "I thought I'd have time and money for travel once I finished school. But then my internship kept me so busy..." She turned to look out over the city. The lights from street signs and buildings nearly blotted out the view of the stars, but one particular pinpoint of light could still be seen to the south. She pointed to it. "I think that star is in the Posungi system. It always seemed so close, like I could visit it over a long weekend. But I never carved out the time."

Chigs huffed in amusement. "You're not missing anything there. I had a couple of missions on Posungi. Nothing but swamp."

She laughed. "Well, it still would've been someplace to visit that wasn't my own home planet. Maybe now that I'm with the rebellion, I'll get to see new places."

He raised his glass. "To traveling the stars."

They sat in comfortable silence for a while, lost in thoughts of travel, until Emmy's eyelids began to droop. She startled awake at the feel of Chigs's powerful arms lifting her from her seat. "What?" she said in a daze, quickly slipping one arm around his neck for support.

"You need to get to bed," he answered as he made his way to the bedroom, carrying her like a child.

She blinked, suddenly wide awake. There was only one bed, and she couldn't help but wonder if he planned to sleep together. *Oh god, yes.* Wait—no! That absolutely could not, would not, happen. She pointed with her free hand towards the chaise lounge as they walked past it. "I can sleep on the sofa."

Chigs ignored her and continued straight to the bedroom. "You'll take the bed," he said, setting her down on the edge of the springy mattress. "I'm sleeping outside, on the balcony."

"Outside?" Emmy repeated in surprise.

He nodded slowly. "Under the stars." He took a step backward, looking uncomfortable. "I really enjoyed talking to you," he muttered softly before turning away. "Goodnight."

Emmy gulped as she caught herself watching his sexy, retreating ass.

"Goodnight," she called after him. Trying to ignore the sudden heat settling low in her belly.

She changed into her pajamas and slipped under the covers, knowing she'd be dreaming of Chigs tonight.

Chapter Eight

Chigs retreated once more to the moonlit balcony and stood at the railing, unable to ignore the scent of Emmy's perfume lingering on him after their dance. His balls ached with pent-up need, but if he was being honest with himself, the attraction went far beyond physical. Emmy's spirit, her intelligence, her passion for helping others, drew him to her. She was easy to talk to and open in a way few were with him. She made him remember the simple joy he'd once found in gazing up at the endless night sky, the days before being a Syndicorp soldier robbed him of his innocence. What would it be like to share adventures with her, to see the universe through her eyes?

He glanced toward the glass doors into the suite, thinking of her lying there on the silken bedsheets. His hand recalled the curve of her hip as they danced. What would it feel like to touch every inch of her bare skin as she arched in pleasure? To trail kisses down her neck and suckle her breasts as she moaned his name? He contemplated going back to the bedroom and slipping beneath the covers with her, knowing full well he couldn't. His destiny was so close now.

Groaning, he pressed the heel of his hand against his swollen cock through his pants. This was madness. He was destined for another. Even now, his true mate could be suffering in a Syndicorp lab. Yet, every fiber of his being strained toward the woman sleeping in the other room. He gripped the balcony railing, torn between his duty to his destined mate and his roiling desire for Emmy.

That infernal ambient music had shifted to a slow, deep beat that made his hips want to tense and thrust, to bury his cock deep inside Emmy's waiting heat. *Uminaq.* He needed a release. Glancing behind him to make sure he was alone, he closed his eyes and dipped one hand inside his pants, glad for the balcony's privacy screen.

His rough fingers circled his shaft, stroking up and down while he pictured Emmy wearing nothing but her delicate perfume. He ran his tongue along his lips, imagining her silken skin, the way her nipples would swell when he sucked them. He could almost hear her moans of pleasure, feel her body trembling under his touch. In his mind, he let his fingers trail down her belly and over the mound of her sex, slipping between her thighs to find her wet and ready.

His balls tightened, but the confines of his pants restricted his strokes, keeping him from release. Frustrated, he glanced behind him once more before opening his fly, letting his engorged cock spring free. His hips bucked with need, and he circled the thick shaft firmly, pumping hard and fast while he imagined Emmy crying out in ecstasy, her channel tightening around him in quivering climax.

That was all it took for him to reach his breaking point, his grip tightening around his cock as he spilled his seed over his hand, gasping Emmy's name.

Guilt flooded him as he came back to reality, panting and spent. He looked down at the mess he'd made. "*Uminaq*," he whispered, wiping his hand on a napkin left from their meal and refastening his pants. "What am I doing?"

He tossed the napkin back onto the tray and took everything to the recycler. It wouldn't do to have Emmy discover any sign of his indiscretion. He shouldn't be having these thoughts about her. Ellam Cua had spoken to him. Had sent those dreams to let him know his mate was out there waiting for him, calling him through their mate bond.

Tovik's question about the need for physical contact to secure a mate bond floated through Chigs's mind, and for the first time, doubt took root in his mind. Was it possible the dream wasn't a sign from Ellam Cua? Kashatok and the others had been cynical. Chigs shook his head. The dream had felt so real, so vivid. And yet… He leaned against the railing of the balcony, thinking back to the images in his dream; the desolate approach to the lab, the rows of chambers, the hazy images of females behind glass. Each woman had looked the same. He sought the memory of his mate's sweet voice calling him, yet all he could hear was Emmy's soft laughter. "Why can't I remember?"

Perhaps his attraction to Emmy was a test to challenge his loyalty and faith. A distraction from his true purpose. He looked out at the horizon, seeking the stars above the lights from the city. He could only see the single bright pinpoint Emmy had pointed to earlier.

It always comes back to Emmy.

Torn between his devotion to a mate he had yet to meet and the feelings in his heart, Chigs muttered, "Ellam Cua, help me. Show me the path I must follow."

The silence that followed only deepened the doubt in his mind. As much as he wanted to remain loyal to his destiny, the connection between him and Emmy was undeniable. The thought of never knowing what could have been between Emmy and himself made him ache with longing.

"Emmy," he breathed, feeling his resolve weaken. "What do I do?"

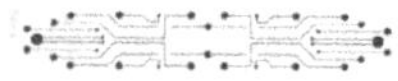

Emmy tossed and turned, unable to quiet her mind. She kept seeing Chigs's face, remembering the feel of his arms around her as he carried her to bed. Her body tingled with longing, desire pulsing between her legs.

Giving up on sleep, she rose and padded into the suite. Perhaps a cup of chamomile tea would help calm her thoughts. As she programmed the replicator, she glanced toward the balcony and spotted Chigs leaning against the railing. His broad back was to her, and one arm moved in front of him in an unmistakable rhythm.

Emmy froze in place, heart pounding. She should leave, give him privacy, but she couldn't tear her gaze away. Who was he picturing? Although logic told her it must be his destined mate, a small part of her wished it was her instead. Her cheeks heated at the thought, and she berated herself for even considering it. Yet the look on his face when he'd left her in the bedroom lingered. Had she imagined the desire in his eyes?

Unable to avert her eyes, Emmy backed toward the bedroom. Her pussy throbbed with need, slick heat coating her inner thighs as he began thrusting his hips. What would it feel like to have him thrust into her like that? She shuddered, rubbing her thighs together until she thought she might climax right there. *Turn away, Emmy.*

It took every ounce of her willpower, but she forced herself to pivot and return to the lonesome bedroom, her heart threatening to pound out of her chest. She threw herself on the bed and buried her face in a pillow, trying to ignore the ache between her legs. But she kept seeing him, kept imagining his hard, muscular body pressed against her. Covering her. Mounting her. She flipped over and let her hand slide over her hardened nipples before dipping her fingers inside her panties to stroke her clit.

Fantasizing about Chigs would only lead to trouble, but she couldn't stop herself. He filled her thoughts. She bit her lip, holding back a moan. Rubbing slow circles around her throbbing button, she imagined it was Chigs's fingers, his cock. The fantasy was so vivid, she could almost feel his hot breath against her neck, hear his low groans in her ear.

Her fingers moved faster as heat coiled within her, the pressure building as she rocked her hips, pleasure spiraling higher. She was close, so close. Just a little more...

She pictured his intense copper eyes boring into hers, full of the desire she'd imagined when he'd tucked her in bed, and her orgasm crashed over her in a blinding wave. For several long moments, she floated in a sea of bliss.

Panting, Emmy pulled her hand free. An uncomfortable mix of relief and anxiety flooded her, and she hugged her pillow close, staring at the ceiling. What was she doing? She'd never felt this sexually attracted to any of her previous love interests, not even Mek or Dafari. And of course, there was the undeniable fact that Chigs was basically already mated. *Falling for the wrong guy, yet again.* But she couldn't deny her attraction. The way his childhood stories made him smile, revealing a youthful innocence behind his tough warrior façade. Or the way her heart constricted when he called her peanut, even though she knew it was part of a script. He would make a wonderful mate when he found his woman.

"Chigs," she whispered into the darkness, as if saying his name would help her make sense of the complicated feelings that had taken root within her heart. But even as Emmy tried to push those feelings away, she knew they wouldn't be easily ignored.

Chapter Nine

The sun had barely risen when Emmy woke, her body still tingling from vivid dreams of Chigs. Her cheeks flushed as she remembered her own actions last night after seeing Chigs on the balcony. She had to get him out of her head, but that would be impossible given their current situation. She was simply going to have to guard her thoughts and emotions and get their mission done as quickly as possible. The sooner he found his mate, the sooner she could move on.

She dressed and ventured from the bedroom to find Chigs already awake and removing a tray from the replicator. Her stomach growled as the scent of bacon wafted toward her.

"Good morning," Chigs said when he spotted her, his voice a little stiff. "I hope you slept well."

Shit. Did he know she'd spied on him? She cleared her throat, hoping the pink early morning light streaming in from the balcony concealed her blush. "I did, thanks."

Liar. She'd tossed and turned for hours, her mind spinning with confused desire. Even looking at him now made her feel all fluttery inside, no matter how many times she reminded herself he could never be hers.

Chigs gestured toward the balcony. "Are you hungry?"

She spotted several platters already arranged on the balcony table. She rarely ate breakfast, but when a hot guy makes you food, you don't say no. "Thanks, that sounds wonderful."

Following him outside, she saw platters filled with heaps of fluffy scrambled eggs, crisp bacon, a large variety of fresh fruit, and warm pastries drizzled with sticky icing. Two tall flutes held bubbly orange juice she was fairly certain must be mimosas, plus two steaming cups of fragrant coffee. Clearly, Chigs knew his way around the food synthesizer.

She pulled out a seat and reached for the coffee, adding a healthy dollop of cream from a small pitcher on the table.

Chigs sat and offered her an empty plate. "I hope this is acceptable. It seems they only offer human food on this menu and wasn't sure what you liked, so I ordered everything from the breakfast options."

"Thanks, it all looks amazing." Accepting the plate, she took eggs, bacon, and one of the decadent pastries. Her craving for Chigs might be unfulfilled, but at least she could indulge in this appetite.

He stabbed a knife into a slice of golden melon and sniffed it. "What do you plan to do today?"

Emmy shifted in her seat. Her nether regions knew exactly what she wanted to do, and she had a fleeting thought about offering to be a friend with benefits. People did that sort of thing all the time, right? *That's not you, Emmy.* And a temporary hook-up certainly wouldn't help their mission.

Forgoing her coffee, she reached for a mimosa, hoping to dull her persistent thoughts. "Maybe some light reading or extra sleep. I'm sure there's something playing on the entertainment channels as well. How about you?"

Chigs seemed to decide the melon was edible and took a bite, chewing slowly before answering. "I'm not great at sitting still. I guess I could practice a few combat moves." He looked around the balcony. "Looks like there's enough room out here."

An image of him bare-chested and sweaty filled her mind. She could almost feel his skin as he pressed her up against a wall and thrust between her legs. Her pussy clenched, and she let out a shaky breath. Dammit, two days locked in close quarters with Chigs might prove her undoing.

She had to clear her head. Pushing her breakfast aside, she said, "Why don't we explore the gardens and grounds? Even newlyweds need a break from..."

Her cheeks ignited like they'd been hit by a blast furnace. Why did everything seem to come back to sex?

Chigs pushed aside his plate as well. "Sounds like a good idea. A walk might help me blow off some energy." He stood and held out his arm. "Shall we go, peanut?"

Her heart fluttered at the endearment, and she had to remind herself it wasn't real. "Better get your holo projector."

"Oh, right." He retrieved it from the charger and placed it around his neck.

Although his human disguise was admittedly handsome, she missed his sexy beard. *Good.* Hopefully, the disguise would help quell her rampant desires.

They left the suite hand in hand, taking the elevator down to the lobby where they exited onto a crushed shell garden path behind the tower. Flowering trees filtered the sun, dappling the ground with shadows and filling the air with pleasant sweetness. Among the lush landscaping between the paths, crystalline sculptures, small fountains, and nooks holding cozy benches beckoned to be explored.

Emmy breathed deep, trying to force the tension from her body, though Chigs's hand firmly enveloping hers was a constant reminder of how complicated her feelings had become. As they strolled, she glanced at him from the corner of her eye, noting the tense set of his shoulders. "What's wrong?" she asked finally.

He gestured toward a fountain shaped like the Syndicorp logo. "Everything here is a reminder of Syndicorp's power."

She looked around at the ever-present Syndicorp propaganda marring the scenery. The advertising was less obtrusive than it had been in the city, but still present everywhere she looked, from holographic projections above the waste receptacles to glittering corporate logos imprinted on the pebbles beneath their feet. "God, I hadn't even noticed."

They continued along the paths, looking for local shops not overtly tied to Syndicorp where Emmy made a point of purchasing a few items. She bought a quaint set of bioluminescent jewelry that glowed pale pink and ordered a piece of quantum-locked sand art to be sent to her parents as a gift. Chigs wanted to buy a miniature bio-dome holding some of the endangered species on Aleigh for Kashatok, but they weren't sure how to get it discretely back to the rebel fleet, so they passed. They stopped for lunch at a small cafe overlooking the azure waves and enjoyed handmade crepes filled with locally grown berries and cream.

In no hurry to get back to their enclosed hotel room and its suggestive AI settings, Emmy suggested they walk along the beach back to the resort.

They strolled along the sand, enjoying the warm sun and fresh air. "I didn't realize how much I missed planet life until now," Emmy said, kicking off her shoes and wading into the water, hiking her dress up to her thighs. "It feels great! Come on in!"

Chigs shook his head and pointed to the holo projector around his neck, glancing nervously at some nearby sunbathers lying in hover loungers near the water.

Emmy waded back out and spoke in a low voice, "Emilryde said the pigment should last a week."

"I'd rather not risk it. You go ahead. I'm glad you get to enjoy it," he said, smiling broadly.

The twinkle in his eyes made her suddenly self-conscious. Yet she couldn't deny liking the way he watched her, especially with no AI to tattle on her rapidly beating heart. She waded back into the water, enjoying the cool waves lapping against her knees and the soft sand between her toes.

They looked for shells together and watched a large green bird dive for fish. When they reached the main path back to the resort tower, she reluctantly waded back out, the hem of her damp skirt clinging to her thighs. Hopefully, the rest of the walk would dry it out. At an outdoor bar at the edge of the beach, a musician played a lively tune a while a few couples danced under the shade of a gazebo. A robotic server handed out drinks to several humans seated on tall stools, while a finofan server carrying a tray scurried toward tables shaded by umbrellas.

Chigs squeezed her hand. "Let's get a drink."

But Emmy stood frozen in place, pulse racing as she stared toward one table where a man sat talking to a woman in a white sundress. His head was bent away from her, but Emmy would recognize that profile anywhere. *Dafari.* She stared hard at the red-haired woman, trying to decide if she knew her. A colleague? A lover?

"What is it?" asked Chigs, following her gaze.

In a cracked whisper, Emmy said, "Dafari is here."

As if hearing his name, Dafari's head swiveled in their direction.

Emmy panicked. She yanked Chigs toward her, standing on tiptoes to mash her lips against his.

Chigs inhaled sharply, then wrapped his strong arms around her and lifted her against his chest, deepening the kiss. His mouth moved hungrily over hers, tongue caressing the seam of her lips until she opened in response.

This was their first full-on kiss, and an explosion of desire stiffened her nipples to aching points against the hard planes of Chigs's chest. One of his big palms slipped down to her ass, holding her against him and sending sparks of pleasure straight to her core. The world around her faded to meaningless chatter, and all that existed was Chigs.

He continued to plunder her mouth, tasting and exploring every inch until she was panting for breath. The sexy musk of his cologne blended with the salty sea air, and his undeniable arousal pressed long and hard against her thigh. She wanted to wrap her legs around his waist and center his heated rod against her pussy, right here, right now.

"Emmy?" Dafari's voice ripped her back to reality.

Chigs broke the kiss and let her slither down his body and back to her feet. Her pulse pounded with unfulfilled desire, and she could barely focus as she turned unsteadily toward her ex-fiancé.

"Oh—hello!" Emmy said, her voice an octave higher than usual. The reality of facing him in person hit home, and she sudden dread filled her. How was she supposed to glean information about the lab when all she wanted to do was run away?

He smiled, his gaze flicking to Chigs before settling back on Emmy. "My friend Irina and I were just about to get another drink. Would you like to join us?"

Chigs saved her from having to respond. "Actually, we were about to enjoy a dance. Perhaps we could join you afterward?"

"Of course," Dafari said, not too subtly taking Chigs's measure. "Whenever you like. We're right over there."

One hand possessively at her waist, Chigs pulled Emmy to the gazebo dance floor where the musician was now playing a slow melody.

"What are you doing?" she asked. "He gave us the perfect opening."

"We need to be sure he believes we're a couple." He pulled her close as she'd showed him on the balcony in their suite. "Besides, I think you need a moment to prepare yourself."

Her heart constricted, and she had to fight back the burning behind her eyes, grateful Chigs understood how she felt. "Thank you."

Bending, he placed a tender kiss to the top of her head, inextricably making the passion she'd felt earlier blossom once again into full-blown lust. *Well, shit.* But she supposed it was better than the angst she'd been feeling at the sight of Dafari. And it would certainly make playing the part of a blushing bride that much easier.

She pressed her cheek against Chigs's chest, keenly aware of his muscular body moving along with hers and how perfectly they fit together. Lyrics floated around them, a ballad about the devotion of a lover's heart. Screw Dafari and his new 'friend.' Emmy might be resigned to never have a true love of her own, but this mission would help Chigs achieve that dream. And that would give her all the satisfaction she could hope for.

The music ended, and Chigs gently squeezed her waist. "Ready, peanut?"

She nodded, lifting her chin in determination. "It's showtime."

CHAPTER TEN

Chigs took stock of Dafari as Emmy led him by the hand to her ex-fiancé's table. The man's artfully mussed blonde hair flopped rakishly over his forehead, and he wore a simple yet immaculate tunic emblazoned with a black and silver Syndicorp logo. He was chatting with the waitress, who beamed at him with obvious flirtation. She laughed and tapped her fingertips against his shoulder before turning away.

Dafari leaned close to his red-headed companion and muttered something, then caught sight of Emmy and Chigs approaching. He seemed to only have eyes for Emmy, and a slow, appreciative smile lifted the corners of his mouth.

You can't have her. The thought came unbidden, but the jealousy burning a hole in Chigs's chest was real. Emmy was amazing. Everything a man could want in a mate, from her generosity and kindness to the undeniable passion smoldering beneath her kiss. Chigs still had a hard-on from their embrace on the dance floor. And the way Dafari was looking at her now made Chigs want to pound the man's supercilious face into mush.

Dafari rose as they drew near, his ice-blue eyes roving suggestively over Emmy's lush curves. "You look more ravishing than ever, Emmy."

"Still a flatterer, I see," replied Emmy, rewarding the man with a small smile. Chigs's fists clenched involuntarily. He knew she was acting, but the thought of her being taken in by Dafari's saccharine charm made his stomach roil.

Dafari grinned in response before turning to thrust a hand toward Chigs. "I'm Dafari."

Chigs accepted Dafari's handshake, squeezing a bit harder than necessary. "Charles Montegue. Emmy's husband."

To his credit, Dafari didn't wince, though he did flex his fingers slightly as he lowered back into his seat.

The red-haired woman extended a hand to Emmy. "I'm Irina. It's good to finally meet you, Emmy. Dafari's told me so much about you."

"Really? Nothing bad, I hope?" Emmy replied with surprising lightness.

"Not at all," the other woman laughed and cut Dafari a reproachful glance. "Sometimes I think he regrets ending it with you."

Emmy's eyebrows shot up and her cheeks pinkened. Clearing her throat, she put a hand to her chest as if flattered. "I'm not sure what to say to that."

Chigs didn't like where this was going. Holding Emmy's chair for her while she sat down, he asked, "Would you like a drink, peanut?"

"A glass of wine would be great," she said.

"I've got this," inserted Dafari, flagging down a nearby finofan server. "A bottle of Chardonnay for the table and an order of calamari." He smiled at Chigs with a challenge in his eyes as the finofan scurried off. "Emmy loves calamari."

Chigs scowled. Maybe a well-aimed punch to the jaw wouldn't be so out of line, after all. He moved his chair close to Emmy's and put an arm around her shoulders. "Emmy loves a lot of things."

Dafari smirked as he leaned back in his chair. "So, how did you two meet?"

"At a bar like this one. I heard her laugh from across the room and knew she was someone special," Chigs beamed at Emmy with full admiration. "It was love at first sight."

"We're on our honeymoon," Emmy said with a nervous laugh, then looked at Irina. "What about you two? How long have you been dating?"

Chigs wondered if she was jealous of the other woman. Might Emmy might still harbor feelings for Dafari? The mere thought of her getting tangled up with this *qumli* again made him see red.

Irina was explaining how a mutual friend at her lab had introduced her to Dafari. "We've only been dating for a month, I think."

"So, you two work together?" asked Emmy.

Dafari eyed her over the rim of his wine glass. "No. I moved on not long after you left."

"Why?" Emmy asked, a little too eagerly. "I thought you were determined to become the lead researcher for that project."

Chigs squeezed her shoulder gently, hoping she understood his unspoken hint to take it slower. She continued staring at her ex intently.

Irina shot Dafari a warning glare and set down her glass. "Let's not discuss work," she said, her voice soft but clear. "It's my first night out in weeks and I'd rather not spoil it with shop talk." Turning a smile on Emmy, she said, "Tell us, what do you two like to do for fun?"

Without waiting for an answer, the woman began recounting a story about a recent trip she and Dafari had taken to the finofan moon. Dafari joined right in, describing their float trip through an underground river system and the exotic creatures they'd seen.

Chigs wasn't great at using his ionic power to sense another person's heartbeat, but he could feel Emmy's pulse racing. He recalled Emmy saying Dafari never had time to travel when they were together. Now it was like the *qumli* was trying to rub it in her face. Chigs cracked his jaw. *If Dafari's no longer with the project, then this conversation is useless.* The mission had turned into a dead end.

"Peanut, we're going to miss the sunset if we don't go now," Chigs said, interrupting one of Dafari's long-winded recounts. He stood and pulled Emmy to her feet, smiling blandly at Dafari. "Thanks for the drink. Perhaps we'll add Finofan to the end of our honeymoon."

Dafari shot to his feet and hurried around the table. "It was great to see you again, Emmy."

It looked as if he was about to hug her, and Chigs felt a growl swell in his chest. He snagged Dafari's hand, forcing the man to back up a step. "Good to put a name to the face, Dafari."

Dafari returned the grip with a firmness that rivaled his own. "Charles." His gaze tracked toward the holo-projector at Chigs's throat, settling there a moment too long. "Good to meet you, too."

Hearts beating double time, Chigs quickly guided Emmy away from the restaurant, forcing himself to keep his gaze focused straight ahead. Did the man suspect something? If Dafari looked hard enough into Chigs's fabricated background, he was bound to find inconsistencies. The entire mission could go sideways in a heartbeat.

As soon as he and Emmy were alone in the elevator to their suite, he turned to her. "I think we've been compromised. We should pack up and leave immediately."

"What do you mean?"

"He looked right at my holo-projector. I think he suspects something."

Emmy's shoulders relaxed, and she laughed. "He was probably just sizing you up. Dafari's very competitive, especially when it comes to women." Her laughter cut off and regret washed over her lovely features. "I'm sorry we didn't get any information that could help us find your mate."

His stomach tightened as he realized he hadn't even been thinking about his mate. He just wanted to get Emmy as far away from here as possible.

The door to the honeymoon suite slid open, and Emmy stepped ahead of him into the soft, post-sunset light flowing in from the suite's balcony doors. The way the pink light bathed her curves took his breath away, and when she turned to him, he was captivated. She'd just faced down the source of a painful memory on his behalf. And here she was, still more concerned about him than herself. He couldn't remember the last time anyone had made him feel so cared for.

As he gazed into Emmy's eyes, his certainty that his dream was a divine calling wavered. What if his interpretation was wrong? The longer he spent with Emmy, the more uncertain he became. It felt like there was something between them, something that would cease to exist if he followed the path ahead.

Ellam Cua, guide me! He was beginning to doubt this entire mission.

He disengaged the holo-projector and ran a hand through his beard. "We're only here because of a vision. I'm wondering if it was only a dream after all."

"Don't discount your dream just yet," Emmy said, hurrying to retrieve her data pad from her luggage. "The SAC units you saw exist—I saw them myself, remember? Before we give up, I'll try to reach out to some of my other colleagues here on Aleigh." She plopped onto the chaise lounge, kicking off her sandals and drawing one bare foot up under her as she perused her contact list.

The sundress she wore left her shoulders bare, and the gentle curls of her hair fanned across her creamy skin. Chigs wanted to run his fingers through it, to press his nose against her throat and inhale her sweetness, to explore the softness of her curves. *I'm going to do it.*

The thought rocked him to the core. Was he actually ready to abandon his vision?

He thought back to the way Emmy had kissed him, how her mouth had opened to his prodding, and her heartbeat had raced against his. On the dance floor, she'd clung to him like she'd meant it. It couldn't all be an act, could it? She had to feel it, too. There was something between them.

He stepped closer to her, his hearts thudding like drums in his chest. "Emmy, I need to tell you something…"

Chapter Eleven

Emmy stared at her list of contacts, wracking her brain for anyone who might've been peripherally involved in Dafari's project. The thought of coming all this way, facing down Dafari, and leaving Aleigh empty-handed made her feel sick. There had to be someone else who could help them. "Here's a lab tech I remember from the project," she muttered. "I wonder if she's still in the area?"

Chigs sat on the chaise next to her and put a warm hand on her forearm.

The shock of his touch sent a shiver through her. Blinking as if from a daze, she lifted her attention to meet his burnished copper eyes.

"I've been thinking—" He exhaled slowly, breath caressing her bare shoulder as he seemed to struggle for words.

She bit her bottom lip, heart filling her throat. Was he giving up on finding his destined mate? She couldn't allow herself to hope for such a thing. She loved how dedicated Chigs was, how loyal, even if it was to another woman. He deserved to find happiness.

He could be happy with me. The thought came unbidden but powerful. A deep yearning unlike any she'd felt before. She wanted to say it out loud. To confess her feelings and throw herself against him. But she kept her lips clamped shut over the words, drawing on every ounce of reserve she'd learned as a therapist. Now wasn't the time for her to speak. It was time for her to listen.

"Would you…" Chigs slid his hand down her arm to take her hand, sending an electric jolt of desire through her.

Oh, God, is he going to say what I think he is? She held her breath, hope making her dizzy.

A loud buzz made her flinch. Chigs shot to his feet, releasing her hand as if he'd been caught committing a crime. A small green light flashed from the com unit on the wall.

Disappointment hit her stomach like a lead weight. All anticipation of confessions, no matter how foolish they might have been, disintegrated between one breath and the next. But what did she expect? She was always drawn to unavailable or uninterested men, and the forbidden Chigs was no exception to that rule. The thought filled her with raging despair. Stupid heart, stupid mission, *stupid buzzer...*

She rose and went to the panel. "It could be Doug," she said, proud her voice didn't tremble. "But just in case, better put your disguise back on."

Chigs nodded, his copper face a shade off-color, and reengaged the holo-projector, resuming his handsome human façade.

Emmy activated the com's small video screen, expecting Doug's familiar cybernetic eye to greet her. "Hello?"

Instead, Dafari's face appeared. "Hello, Emmy."

Every muscle in her body tightened. "Dafari? How did you find me?"

"You said you were on your honeymoon," he said with a smirk. "So I called every hotel in the area and asked for the honeymoon suite until I reached you."

Emmy frowned. Tracking her down must have taken some effort. *Why is he calling?* She recalled Irina mentioning that he regretted breaking up with her. Certainly it wasn't that, was it? Though he had been very flattering over drinks… Perhaps she should play along. Even if he didn't work at the lab anymore, he might still have a nugget of information they could use.

She smiled sweetly, forcing herself to relax and lean close to the screen. "Well, you found me," she replied, her voice low and sultry. "Now what?"

"I can't stop thinking about you. I regret how everything went down between us, but I couldn't get into it with Irina there."

He wants to get back together? Seriously? She tried not to let the surprise register on her face. This could be her opening, but she had to tread carefully if she was to get any information. Dafari knew how to stay close-lipped about his projects. "You know why I had to end our relationship," she said softly. "My feelings haven't changed."

"Let's talk about it more in private," Dafari said, glancing over his shoulder as if worried he might be overheard. "Meet me at the Velvet Enigma tonight at eleven."

She pursed her lips, then nodded. "Okay."

"Come alone," Dafari added, then disconnected.

Emmy stared at the blank screen, pulse whooshing in her ears. After taking a calming breath, she turned to look at Chigs, who stood with his arms crossed.

"Why did you agree to meet him?" he asked, his voice nearly a growl. "He doesn't work at the lab."

She frowned. "But he did for a long time. If he has any information at all, it's worth checking out. We can't abandon this mission if there's even a scrap of a chance to salvage it. Not yet."

"I'm telling you, he suspects something. He knows we're on our honeymoon, yet asked to see you alone."

"I think he might hope he can win me back." Emmy bit her lip, repulsed by the idea but willing to play along for the sake of the mission.

The muscles in Chigs's jaw bulged. "What if I'm right and it's a trap?"

"You're being paranoid." She shook her head. "Our breakup may have been ugly, but Dafari wouldn't set me up." He'd chosen his work over their relationship, but Dafari would never actually sacrifice her for his own advancement.

"I won't let you take the risk. It's not worth it."

"I'm willing to do it, Chigs. Remember, more than just your mate is at stake here—there were other denaidans in those SAC units."

She applied fresh makeup and styled her hair in loose waves that cascaded down her back. Once she was happy with her appearance, she took a fortifying breath and entered the living area where Chigs sat waiting.

He immediately stood, gaze traveling slowly down her body and back up again. "Wow." His throat moved in a swallow. "You're magnificent."

"Thank you," she said, feeling truly beautiful despite the heat crawling over her cheeks.

Chigs held out his arm, and she took it, allowing him to escort her through the lobby to the main entrance. Hailing her a hover transport, he helped her into the passenger compartment. "Remember, I'll be right behind you."

As the car accelerated away, Emmy watched through the window until he disappeared from sight. Then she settled back against the seat, breathing slowly to settle her nerves. She did not know what to expect when she met Dafari, but she was determined to keep her wits about her.

CHAPTER TWELVE

Long shadows flickered through the windows of Chigs's transport as he zipped between the buildings. He'd lost sight of Emmy in the flow of traffic, and his hearts thudded rapidly against his ribs. He checked his data pad, verifying the tracker was working. Emmy's dot moved steadily along the road ahead.

He looked out at the city lights peppered with corporate advertising. He didn't trust Dafari, not one bit, especially when it came to Emmy. Not only was the man an obvious Syndicorp supporter, Chigs had seen the desire in the man's gaze when they'd shared drinks earlier. It had been blatantly obvious the *qumli* was trying to impress Emmy—despite the fact his new girlfriend sat right beside him.

Chigs knew he had no right to be jealous, but at some point, his feelings for Emmy had crossed a line, and now it felt there was no turning back. He'd been ready to confess his desire for her this afternoon, to give up on his vision. Then Dafari had called, reopening their path forward. Guilt squeezed Chigs's chest. If Ellam Cua had picked his perfect mate and shown him the path to find her, then it was wrong to want Emmy. But no matter how much he tried to reassert his faith, he couldn't stop yearning for what might have been.

Ahead, he spotted a towering building at least eighty stories high with a gold sign out front proclaiming it as the Velvet Enigma. The building's exterior was a smooth, matte black that seemed to absorb the light around it like a black hole, as if daring anyone to penetrate the secret dealings inside, and several transports lined up out front, allowing patrons to step out under the massive gold awning leading up to the entry.

He didn't need the tracker to verify Emmy's diminutive, red-clad figure stepping from a transport as he passed by. He directed his transport to pull to the curb a few blocks away before hurrying to the bar after her. A doorman dressed in smart black and gold livery held open the door to the lobby, where soft music played. The air lingered with the scent of expensive cologne.

A woman with curly yellow locks and dark brown skin stood behind a dark marble hostess counter. "Welcome to Velvet Enigma," she greeted with a blinding white smile. "Would you like to experience our newest theme, a visit to the ancient city of Sula'terran?"

"No, thank you," said Chigs, stepping toward the tables he could see in the bar behind her. "I'm meeting someone."

The hostess stepped from behind the counter, politely but assertively blocking his way. "The guest's name, please?"

He gave her what he hoped was a charming smile. "I'm sure I can find her, thanks."

"I'm sorry, sir, but the privacy of our guests is of the utmost importance. I can't let you in without a reservation." She blinked, revealing the flash of a cybernetic connection embedded in her eye. Alerting security? Emmy had mentioned that this place was known for its clandestine meetings.

Chigs lowered his head, speaking to the hostess in a confidential tone. "I'm here to meet the woman in a red dress who arrived just before me." He reached into his pocket and pulled out a credit chip. "I'll make it worth your while if you just point me in the right direction."

The woman looked at the credit chip with derision. "The buy-in for our VIP level is ten thousand."

Of course Dafari would want to meet in the VIP level—he wanted to impress Emmy. Luckily, with Doug's ability to forge nearly infinite resources, Chigs would have no trouble competing. He winked at the hostess. "Not a problem. But I'm only in town for a night, so if we could speed things up…"

The woman's expression shifted to one of calculation. "There's also the matter of the review board… They only meet once a month."

Keeping a smile plastered to his face, Chigs said, "You seem to know a lot about the application process." He pulled a handful of credits from his pocket. "Perhaps we can come to some sort of arrangement?"

"If you can transfer the ten thousand right away, I think we can make something work," she said, pulling a tiny data pad from the bodice of her dress.

Without hesitation, Chigs transferred the credits, knowing full well they'd never reach the review board. Once the transfer was confirmed, the hostess tucked the data pad back into her dress and escorted him into the dimly lit bar. Low-hanging chandeliers cast intimate pools of light over tables surrounded by stylized velvet chairs where men and women in tailored suits and elegant gowns sipped on exotic cocktails. An escalator in the center of the room rose toward the upper levels, its entry guarded by two burly security officers, but the hostess bypassed it, heading for a velvet curtain to one side of the bar where two more security officers stood watch.

The hostess muttered a few words to one of them, passing over a few credits, and he pulled the curtain aside, allowing access. Beyond the curtain, an alcove held a gleaming metal elevator door.

The hostess stepped through and keyed an access code into the control panel. "This will take you directly to the VIP level where you'll have full access," she said. "However, I must warn you that the other levels require a pass. Any suspicious behavior, and you'll be escorted out immediately." As the elevator doors slid open, she turned to him and smiled. "Enjoy your evening, sir."

Chigs entered the car, and when he turned, he found the doors sliding closed, leaving him alone in the sterile metal cube. There didn't appear to be a control panel inside the car, and his belly dropped as he began to rise. He pulled his data pad from his breast pocket. At least he was alone now, so he could check the tracker.

A blank screen met his gaze. Scowling, he restarted the device, but the screen remained blank. *Anaq.* The Velvet

Enigma must be running a signal jammer; not surprising considering the hostess's insistence on guest privacy. Momentarily worried it might also jam his holo-projector, he glanced at his reflection in the metal doors, relieved to find he still looked human. Losing the tracker simply meant he needed to find Emmy on his own. Hopefully, the hostess had pointed him in the right direction.

The elevator came to a halt, and the doors slid open. He was nearly bowled over by a crashing wave of sound, color, and smell. Before him, a massive room was filled with undulating bodies, all in various states of undress. The heavy musk of sex choked the air.

His mouth fell open. *Dafari brought Emmy here?* The man really must be depraved. Had Emmy expected this? The thought made Chigs's stomach churn. He knew little about Emmy's previous relationship other than she claimed the breakup had been ugly. Now his mind replayed the way she'd laughed at Dafari's flattery and his fleeting suspicion that she might still have feelings for her ex.

He shook his head. No. Not his Emmy. This wasn't her scene. He felt that in his soul. But how far would she be willing to go to get information about the lab? She was as determined as he was to follow through with the mission—perhaps even more so. He needed to put a stop to this before things went too far.

Stepping off the elevator, Chigs scanned the room for any sign of Emmy or her red dress. Besides humans, he saw species from across the galaxy. Enayshuans sheened in body powder, saluqan with lavender skin and iridescent veins, finofan with colorful flared ear frills, and even a massive, six-legged yanipa-nimayu. It was an orgy the likes of which he'd never imagined. *Ellam Cua, where's Emmy?*

A tentacle-faced posungi female locked eyes with him and rose from a pool of glistening liquid, all eight of her pointed orange nipples dangling with piercings. "You're new here, aren't you?" she said in a phlegmy voice, facial tentacles writhing. She slid one hand along the glistening curve of her hip suggestively. "How about you let me show you around?"

He swallowed thickly. Posungi were cold-blooded humanoid egg layers, but were known to enjoy copulating with warm-blooded companions. His dick shriveled at the mere idea. Hoping to divert her intention, he pulled a credit chip from his pocket. "Actually, I'm looking for a woman in a red dress. Have you seen her?"

The posungi sidled closer to him. Before he could blink, her tentacles shot out and swept the credit off his palm, stashing it Ellam Cua knew where. Then she looped her arm through his. "Come with me."

Every inch of his skin wanted to peel away from the posungi's clammy touch, but he allowed her to guide him through the crowd, stepping around bodies and evading groping hands. Scattered clothing included more Syndicorp uniforms than he'd care to count.

The room was filled with all sorts of erotic furniture and fixtures, from chairs of various heights and shapes to plush pillows in every imaginable color. In the center of the room, a pair of swings hung from ceiling chains, suspending two couples swaying in wild acts of pleasure. Tucked away in alcoves in the walls, padded platforms surrounded by mirrors created what appeared to be an infinite number of thrusting, gyrating sex acts. Other pieces of equipment like chains, floggers, bondage masks, and vibrators rested on scattered shelves and tables about the space.

His posungi escort halted and pointed to a woman lying on her back in one alcove, red dress bunched around her waist. Two enayshuan men pleasured her with their mouths, while a third human male jacked off while he watched.

"Shall we join them?" gurgled the posungi.

Chigs felt like he couldn't breathe. He stepped closer, dreading what he was about to see past the bunched up red dress. In one of the many mirrors, he caught sight of the woman's face, chin thrust upward as she gasped in pleasure, hands gripping the sides of her short blond hair.

He released a shaky breath. "That's not her."

The posungi shrugged. "Well, that's the only woman in red who came in here tonight."

He glanced out over the crowd. Emmy wasn't here. He could sense it. The hostess had sent him after the wrong red dress. Which meant he needed to get out of here and somehow find Emmy without the tracker. But the hostess had already warned him the other levels required a separate pass.

Reaching into a pocket, he withdrew a handful of credits. "Can you point me to the stairs?"

"This is a secure level. The stairwell is locked."

"Let me worry about that. I just need to know where they are."

She shrugged, and the credits once more disappeared among her tentacles. Turning, she began walking through the throng, stopping several paces away from a wall with a gauzy curtain where a human with gleaming metal arms stood watch. "There. Behind the curtain."

A chill ran down Chigs' spine. The man was a cyborg, a deadly adversary, even for a denaidan. He was aware Syndicorp bigwigs hired them out as bodyguards, but he'd never met one outside of Doug and his crew. Glancing around, he spotted several more cyborgs staged around the perimeter, including one near the elevator, who he'd missed in his shock at seeing the orgy.

The posungi turned to leave, but he caught her arm. "Wait."

"Change your mind, honey?" One of her facial tentacles looped out to trail a cold, wet line down his chest. It froze as it contacted his beard. Her orange eyes widened as she stared at the empty space below his chin.

Uminaq. Chigs seized her hand, dragging her a few steps away from the guard. "Don't say a word."

She pulled free of his grip, a slimy tongue snaking between her lips as she assessed him. "Oh, I can be discreet. For a price."

Chigs dug out more credits. "I also need you to cause a distraction."

She laughed thickly. "This entire room is a distraction."

"You know what I mean."

She eyed the credits again. "If I cause trouble, they'll punish me. Possibly for weeks. You need to make it worth my while."

He frowned, wondering if she was a slave. Syndicorp didn't publicly condone slavery, but he knew from experience that there was still a market. *You don't have time to worry about that.* Right now, he needed to get out of here and find Emmy. He retrieved the remainder of his credits and held them out.

The posungi grinned and took the money, her tentacles undulating as if they were about to launch her into flight. "Give me a few minutes and you'll have your distraction."

Turning, she sauntered back into the crowd.

Praying she'd keep her word, Chigs turned his attention back to the guard near the stairwell. He wasn't sure what the posungi had in mind, but he needed to be ready. Pretending to examine the couples for a chance to join in, he moved closer.

A minute later, there was an earsplitting shriek from somewhere on the other side of the room. Everyone stopped what they were doing and looked around in confusion.

The guard moved away from the door, clearly intending to investigate if there was trouble. Not wasting a second, Chigs hurried forward and pressed his hand to the exit's control panel, using a quick ionic pulse to short-out the lock. Pushing into the stairwell, he closed the door behind him and breathed a sigh of relief. Now he just had to hurry and find Emmy.

CHAPTER THIRTEEN

Emmy resisted the urge to look around for Chigs as the hostess led her past two burly bouncers and up a series of escalators, each one guarded by a pair of bouncers. She'd never been to the Velvet Enigma, and everywhere she looked there was something new and exciting to take in. One level was decorated with vintage furniture and played old-school music. Another blasted a quick, pulsating beat, the strobe-lit dance floor packed with gyrating bodies. Yet another held patrons singing karaoke at the top of their lungs.

Finally, they stopped on a floor decorated in dimly lit neon columns filled with slowly rising bubbles and low, chrome-polished tables surrounded by plush leather seats. The hostess led her between the tables, the buzz of conversations nearly overriding the soft electronic music filling the bar.

Glancing around, Emmy noted the high number of Syndicorp uniforms present. A thread of worry wove its way through her chest. Maybe Chigs's prediction about this being a trap was true. She hesitated, considering if the risk would be worth it, but Dafari had already spotted her from a table near the bar and rose to greet her. Steeling her resolve, she walked straight toward him.

"Emmy, my love," Dafari purred, his voice low and seductive. "You look absolutely stunning." He attempted to guide her into the seat next to him, but she skirted his hand and chose the spot across the table.

She'd agreed to this meeting under the pretext of possibly rekindling their relationship, but no matter how hard she tried, she couldn't bring herself to pretend. "What do you want, Dafari? Charles isn't happy I'm here with you."

With a tight smile, he sat, picking up his vivid green cocktail. "Can I buy you a drink?"

"Where's your girlfriend?" she asked pointedly, ignoring his offer.

"Ah," he said, taking a sip from his glass. "I wouldn't exactly call Irina my girlfriend. Irina is... just someone I spend time with." He leaned forward, staring intently into her face. "Truthfully, I've always regretted the way things ended between us."

"Is that so?" Emmy's lip wanted to curl, but she kept her face straight. He was obviously trying to manipulate her, as usual. What in the hell had she ever seen in him? She crossed her arms. "I bumped into a mutual acquaintance on Whylon Station," she said coolly. "It sounds like you have an interesting perspective about what really happened during our breakup."

His brows shot up. "I was merely trying to save your career after you disappeared. I told people you needed to regroup after ending our relationship. Why didn't you accept any of the job offers I arranged for you?"

She frowned. She hadn't realized the offers had been because of him. "Why would you do that for me?"

"Because I still care about you." His gaze seemed to search hers for any sign of reciprocation.

"I'm happily married now." She crossed her arms. "Charles and I are going to live on Jarboa. He owns a plantation there."

Dafari's eyebrows rose in surprise, but he quickly recovered. "A farmer's wife? I never would've imagined that for you, Emmy."

"He's not a farmer," Emmy said in a cold tone. "He's a decorated war hero, retiring from service with honors." She glanced around the bar, hoping Chigs had found her by now. She could use his grounding influence. But he was nowhere in sight.

"You and I were a great team, Emmy," Dafari said softly. "We could be that again."

Her anger sparked at his audacity. "How dare you even suggest that, especially after everything you put me through? You never truly loved me, Dafari. Your career always came first." She glared at him, voice rising slightly. "Now tell me why you really asked me to meet you here."

Dafari hesitated, his attention darting around the room before finally relenting. Reaching into his breast pocket, he produced a small data chip and slid it across the table. "When you left, you said you wanted to expose the project. Assuming you still do, I want to help you."

Emmy stared at him, not daring to even glance at the chip on the table between them. She scanned the dimly lit bar, heart pounding in anticipation of trouble. "Why are you offering me this?" she whispered.

Dafari leaned back as if this was the most comfortable conversation in the world. "You could say I've had a change of heart."

Emmy studied him with narrowed eyes. "Why?" she insisted again.

"That bastard running things cut me out." A grimace of anger crossed his face before he resumed a placid expression. "I want the project to come crashing down around his head."

Now things made more sense. Dafari's fragile ego had been damaged. He was probably thinking that if he couldn't be involved, he'd make sure nobody else was, either. "Why don't you just expose it yourself?"

He took another sip of his drink, looking at her over the rim of the glass. "Because, unlike you, I want to stay in Syndicorp's good graces."

Of course he does. Just because he was ready to expose this project didn't mean he'd suddenly grown a conscience. With a flick of her wrist, she slid the chip into her handbag and stood. As she turned to leave, Dafari caught her hand.

"Don't sit on this, Emmy. The lab could relocate at any time." Dropping her hand, he turned away as if in dismissal, signaling the waitress for another drink.

Once upon a time, the gesture would've stung. Now she was relieved to be leaving him behind. *To think I almost trapped myself in marriage to him.* Her parents had been right.

As Emmy walked determinedly towards the escalator, her newfound sense of liberation made her steps feel lighter. After this mission was over, she could finally forget about Dafari. She had a family among the rebels, people who actually cared about her. Just the thought of Chigs finding happiness with his mate made her smile, though a bit sadly. Their time together on this mission had been wonderful, and although she couldn't have Chigs for her own, she had a new friend in him.

As if summoned by her thoughts, the sound of Chigs's voice floated up the escalator. "I told you already. I'm just looking for my table."

She reached the bottom to find him gripped between two brawny bouncers, fists curled as if ready to throw a punch. He spotted her and his expression instantly brightened. "There she is!"

The bouncer looked at Emmy. "He's with you?"

Emmy nodded, and the bouncers stepped back and bowed their heads apologetically. "Sorry for the misunderstanding," one of them said.

She smiled indulgently. "It's all right. We're just leaving now, anyway."

Chigs hooked a possessive arm around her waist. "Let's get the hell out of here," he said firmly, steering them toward the exit.

He set a pace that nearly had her running beside him, and by the time they reached the curb, she was slightly out of breath. "Chigs, what's going on?"

He summoned a transport and guided her inside, waiting until they were speeding away to describe his adventure to the penthouse. "I never want to see a naked posungi ever again," he stated. "And I'm not even going to talk about what the yanipa-nimayu was doing."

Emmy giggled and shuddered at the same time. "That sounds… traumatizing?"

He shook his head. "You have no idea. Speaking of traumatizing, did you meet Dafari?"

She held up the data chip, realizing she didn't feel upset at all. She felt good. Energized. "He gave me this. I guess he's pissed about getting booted from the project, so he's hoping we can cause some trouble."

Chigs narrowed his eyes. "This feels too easy. I don't trust him."

"You're right to be cautious, but I know Dafari well enough to gauge his intentions. I believe he was sincere."

She pressed the chip into Chigs's hand, finding the next words difficult to force past her lips. "This could finally lead you to your mate."

Sighing, Chigs closed his fingers around the chip. "All right, we'll go through it and see what we can find." For a lingering moment, his eyes roamed her face, as if trying to memorize her features. "Thank you for all you've done, Emmy. I'll be glad to get off this planet." Then he turned to stare out the window.

A mix of conflicting emotions filled Emmy's throat, and she turned to stare out her own window. For the first time, she realized this meant her mission with Chigs was over. They'd no longer be spending time together one-on-one. He and the other denaidans would start planning a raid on the lab along with a rescue mission for Chigs's mate and the other denaidan females. Emmy's heart ached as she realized how much she was going to miss the warmth of intimacy that had ignited between them.

You'll still see him on board the ship, she reminded herself. *We're friends now.*

But she wanted to be more than friends. And that would never happen.

The transport pulled up to the hotel, and Chigs offered a gentlemanly hand to help her out. They still had to play the part of newlyweds until they got off the planet, so walked to the elevator arm-in-arm. Though she smiled and tried to behave like she was in love, she had to bite her lower lip to keep it from trembling.

Chapter Fourteen

Chigs knew they needed to get the data chip back to the *Icarus* as soon as possible and work on a plan to rescue the women, but he was sorely tempted to prolong their stay on Aleigh. Thoughts of the future weighed heavily on him—a future that wouldn't include Emmy—and he wasn't ready to move on.

Emmy, however, seemed all too eager to leave. "The sooner we get the chip to Doug for decryption, the better," she announced while stuffing the last of her clothing into her suitcase. "Dafari hinted that the lab might move soon."

The honeymoon suite was brightly lit, as if trying to chase his uncertainty back into the darkness where it belonged. Yet it was becoming more and more impossible for him to believe his true mate was among the women at the lab. Not when a mere glance from Emmy sent both his hearts into overdrive.

He grabbed his bag and hurried toward the elevator after Emmy, reaching for her suitcase. "Let me carry that." When she opened her mouth to protest, he insisted, "You're still my beloved bride until we get back to the *Icarus*."

What looked like a flash of pain filled her eyes, but she nodded tersely, turning away to stare at the elevator doors. "Right. We need to keep up the ruse a little while longer."

The ruse. His chest felt tight as they rode down to the lobby in silence. They caught a ride to the spaceport and booked passage on a cargo carrier scheduled for a turn-and-burn to Jarboa, maintaining their story of returning home. From Jarboa, they'd grab a shuttle and rendezvous with the *Icarus* just outside Syndicorp space. The carrier was leaving immediately, forcing them to rush down a narrow gray corridor to reach their minuscule cabin before liftoff. Two beat up nav-grav seats took up most of the space, their dull gray fabric frayed and stained, along with a small lavatory and an overhead luggage rack that forced Chigs to stoop. He secured their suitcases and turned to find Emmy glowering at the chairs.

"I'm not looking forward to this," she said. "These units look like they were salvaged from a dump. You think they actually work?"

"I can extend my ionic shielding to reduce the effect of the jump for you." He held out a hand and moved toward the nearest seat. "Let's double up." The trip would only take them a day, but would require three burns in rapid succession. He wasn't looking forward to the taxing itinerary, but at least he had his ionic power to shield him from the worst of it. She'd only have the nav-grav unit.

Emmy's eyes widened, and for a moment he thought she might accept. But then she shook her head. "No, I can handle it."

"Have you ever actually experienced a turn-and-burn?" he asked. "It can be excruciating for humans."

She bit her lower lip and again eyed the dilapidated seats. "No."

He stepped closer and took her hand. "Let me help." He sat and pulled her onto his lap. A spark of heat arced between them as her curves settled against him.

"Chigs, I don't think—" The deck shuddered, making her words wobble as the ship left the spaceport.

He tightened his arms around her protectively. "This isn't a luxury cruise liner, Emmy. You need to be functional when we reach the *Icarus*. Everyone will want to hear what happened with Dafari."

She stopped struggling and took a deep breath, though she remained rigid. "I suppose. But you need to keep your strength so you can rescue your mate."

The reminder echoed inside him like a hollow drum. "Let me worry about that."

The announcement to prepare for burn came over the intercom, ending the argument. Chigs increased the intensity of his ionic shielding to create a cocoon of protection around them. Even so, the sensation of space folding in on itself invaded his senses, and lethargy spread to his limbs like a drunken wave. He closed his eyes, riding it out. It was a good thing he'd insisted on holding Emmy, because these ancient nav-grav units were almost useless.

Emmy swayed and let her head fall back against his chest, obviously feeling the effects as well. He held her firmly but gently, all too aware of the bare skin of her arms beneath his fingertips. Unable to resist, he lowered his cheek against her hair, breathing deeply. Soft floral notes blended with a scent that was all female—all Emmy.

The timeline of a burn was an indefinite thing, and it seemed to both last forever and be over too soon. As the ship resumed normal propulsion, the pressure against his ionic shielding eased and he was able to relax his control. He kept his arms loosely around Emmy, though, unwilling to let her go quite yet. Holding her satisfied him in a way he'd never imagined possible.

Eventually, Emmy roused and stood. "Thank you. That really helped." She looked at him with concern. "How are you doing?"

"I'm great. Don't worry about me." His hands itched to grasp her hips and pull her back onto his lap, but he stood and stretched. "The next burn is in just a few minutes. Do you need privacy for a moment?" He gestured toward the small lavatory.

"No, but a drink of water might be nice."

Happy to have a task, he hurried to the ship's galley and located a packet of water, making it back to their cabin with a few minutes to spare. "Here you are."

She took several long swallows before offering it back. "Do you need any?"

He wasn't thirsty, but took a sip anyway. "Thank you."

She finished the packet and wedged it into the luggage rack until they could find a recycler.

"Ready?" he asked, settling into the nav-grav seat and holding out a hand once more.

This time she settled into his lap more readily, her body molding against his like it was meant to be there. He wrapped both arms around her softness and raised his shielding as the countdown to burn began. The dizziness came and went once more, this time with an added prickle of heat. Within the cocoon of his ionic shielding, his and Emmy's scents mingled into an intoxicating blend of desire, and he couldn't stop his cock from hardening against her ass.

Long moments after the burn was complete, he remained frozen with his arms lockout around her, his breathing shallow, thighs tense. He couldn't seem to make himself let go.

Emmy didn't seem to be in any hurry to stand, either. Ever so slowly, she turned to look over her shoulder at him, lips but a breath from his. It was all too much. Mission be damned. He couldn't resist this any longer. Closing the distance, Chigs brushed his mouth against hers. Her lips parted in invitation, and she leaned into the kiss, igniting a plasma burn through his veins. He slid his tongue over hers, tasting her sweetness.

So sweet. So soft. So *mine*.

He gripped her tighter, crushing her softness against his chest.

Her scent spiked with arousal. Lips still locked with his, she squirmed, grinding her ass against his hardening cock. Twisting so she sat semi-sideways, she shrugged one hand free of his embrace to grasp the back of his neck and pull him closer.

He half groaned, half growled, probing deeper into her mouth and letting one hand slide over her breast. Her nipple hardened to a point through the fabric of her shirt, and he pinched it gently, eliciting a gasp from her that only made him crave more. He wanted to hear her cry his name in ecstasy.

Emmy reached down with her free hand and rubbed the thick shaft of his cock through his pants. The pressure made his balls ache with pent-up need. She rolled her hips against his cock again, parting her thighs as if in invitation.

Uminaq, yes. His hand left her breast and slipped into the waistband of her pants, delving beneath her panties to find her hot and wet. He cupped her mound, one finger slipping easily between her slick folds. He began moving in a slow circle, stroking the velvety inner lips and gliding over her swelling clit.

A low moan welled in her throat. She tilted her hips toward him, legs wide and inviting. He dipped one finger into her channel, loving the tight heat clenched around him. Adding a second finger, he slid in and out while flicking his thumb over her clit.

She whimpered, hand fumbling under her hip toward the closure of his fly. Much as he wanted her to free him, he was intent on one thing now, and made no move to assist. "Come for me," he murmured against her lips as he increased his rhythm, plunging his fingers as deep as they would go. She pulsed against his hand and moaned, bucking to meet his penetrating thrusts.

He curled his fingers, catching the sensitive ridges deep inside her until she cried out, "Chigs!"

Her walls spasmed, but he continued thrusting until her shudders subsided. She slumped back against his chest, panting. "Oh, my God."

He cradled her against him, breathing shallowly. His balls ached, but he was used to restraining himself; he hadn't been with a woman since before the destruction of his planet. Right now, he was content to enjoy the aftermath of Emmy's pleasure. He gently moved a lock of hair that had been stuck to her flushed cheek and feathered kisses against her temple.

Emmy inhaled deeply, one palm roaming up his chest to his beard, running along his jaw. He angled his head down, preparing for another kiss, when she sat up suddenly, opening a cold chasm between their bodies. Her eyes were wide as she shot to her feet and turned to face him. "We can't... that can't happen again."

Chigs's chest tightened as the full realization of the moment hit him. *Ellam Cua, what am I doing?*

CHAPTER FIFTEEN

Chigs scrubbed a hand over his scalp, emotions and desires ricocheting through his mind like enemy crossfire. "Of course," he agreed hoarsely.

He was supposed to be finding his mate, not fooling around with Emmy. But duty and logic did nothing to remove his desire.

Emmy took several unsteady steps back and plunked down in the other nav-grav seat, buckling herself in without glancing his way again. The final burn and short remainder of their carrier ride was made in near silence, and by the time they reached the small spaceport on Jarboa, Emmy'd resumed her former aloof persona.

It was nighttime when they arrived, and beyond the running lights of the cargo ship, the austere landing pad was lit only by a single tall post with a bulb of sickly orangish light glowing at its apex. Chigs grabbed their luggage and led the way through the shadows toward a dilapidated hangar at the other edge of the tarmac. Doug had acquired a small, undocumented shuttle off the dark web so Chigs could discretely fly them to meet the *Icarus*.

Shoving the hangar door aside with a teeth-grating screech, Chigs grimaced at the sight of a vessel that looked like it had come from the same dump as the nav-grav seats in the cargo carrier. The nose was slightly buckled, and the under panels near the thrusters were dark and sooty. He'd only piloted solo a handful of times, and this bucket of rust barely looked space-worthy.

Not wanting Emmy to worry, he entered the code to the hatch and stowed the luggage in stoic silence before assuming the pilot's seat. Emmy had already buckled into the co-pilot seat and sat with her head back and her eyes closed, obviously exhausted from the final burn on the cargo ship.

Reminded of why she'd chosen to endure that awful nav-grav seat, he set his jaw and ignored the acid burning in his stomach, focusing on his flight check. After going over the system three times, he finally lifted them off the tarmac with a teeth-rattling thrust. By the time they set down in the *Icarus's* shuttle bay and Chigs opened the hatch, he was in no mood to see Tovik sprinting toward them.

"You're back!" Tovik shouted, his bare feet slapping across the deck. "Did you get the information? I want to hear all about Aleigh."

"Later, kid. I'm tired."

Tovik leaned to peer around Chigs into the shuttle. "Where's Emmy? Oh, there she is!" Tovik elbowed past Chigs to offer her an arm. "*Assirpaa!* You look beat."

Chigs reined in his urge to grab Tovik by the scruff and toss him from the shuttle. The mission was over; playing the part of a possessive husband was no longer his duty. But his aching hearts and churning stomach argued differently.

"I see the disguise is still working," called Emilryde from the base of the shuttle ramp.

Chigs realized his holo-projector was still running and quickly turned it off, jerking the chain from his neck and stalking down the ramp. He thrust the projector toward the cyborg. "Like a charm."

Emilryde accepted it with a confused look, but more crew members had arrived and began peppering Chigs with questions. He answered tersely, keeping an eye on Emmy as Tovik escorted her from the shuttle. She joined the crew, smiling and laughing, apparently getting a second wind. Even so, Chigs sensed tension in the way she held herself, and got the feeling she was making an effort not to look at him.

Rust thudded through the crowd, cybernetic gaze focused on Emmy, and Chigs scowled, preparing to step in. The cyborgs were okay as a whole, but Rust could turn volatile for no apparent reason.

"Here." Rust held a small wrapped box toward Emmy and muttered something Chigs couldn't understand.

Emmy's face lit up, and she accepted the gift, placing a hand on Rust's forearm in a way that made Chigs wonder if she and Rust were in a relationship—or if Emmy was in a relationship with anyone else, for that matter. He'd never thought to inquire, but the mere idea made him grit his teeth.

A cybernetic hand settled on his shoulder. "So, where's the chip?" Doug asked.

Chigs dug into his pocket and handed him the small chip, feeling guilty that he hoped the data was corrupted. "Here. Sure hope that Dafari guy isn't taking us for a ride."

Doug nodded. "I'll get to decrypting it immediately."

"You're probably starving," Twerp called over the rumble of conversation, rolling back and forth noisily on her treads. "I've been practicing my cooking skills if anyone would care to join me in the mess hall."

Chigs was too pent up with frustration to eat. Exhausted as he was from the turn-and-burns, he needed to blow off some steam. He shrugged off the invitation and headed for the sparring gym.

His boots echoed against the metallic floor as he strode down the corridor, trying to shake off his mood. He tried reminding himself he should be happy they were one step closer to rescuing his mate. But it was impossible to care for someone he'd never even met when his feelings were so wrapped up in Emmy.

He reached the sparring deck and found it empty. The mats were worn from years of combat practice, and frayed punching bags hung from the ceiling, swaying slightly in the recycled air. Chigs walked over to the weapons rack and chose a staff, testing its balance.

He'd always liked this place, had always found solace in focusing solely on the physicality of fighting. He needed that release now more than ever as he grappled with his conflicting emotions. Duty bound him to the divine message of Ellam Cua. But how was he supposed to fall in love with another woman when his heart longed for Emmy?

"You gonna hit something or just stand there and brood?" Kashatok's voice broke Chigs from his reverie.

Turning, he saw his tall, bearded friend leaning against a second weapon rack, a wry smile playing at the corners of his mouth. How long had Kashatok been standing there? "Hit something," Chigs said, swinging his staff. "Want to volunteer?"

Kashatok laughed and picked up a staff of his own. "I dare you to try, *iluq*."

They squared off, and Chigs launched into a series of strikes, whipping the staff through the air. Each crack against Kashatok's parry vibrated through his hands, easing the tension in his shoulders. But no amount of exertion could quiet the dilemma in his head.

Kashatok landed a blow against the back of his hand, leaving Chigs's knuckles throbbing. "Where's your mind?" asked his friend. "It's obviously not in this fight."

Chigs spun, attempting to sweep Kashatok's feet out from under him. His friend knew him too well. "This mission has me questioning everything."

Using a burst of ionic power, Kashatok leaped over Chigs's attack, landing nimbly against the mat. "This is about Emmy, isn't it?"

"I can't get her out of my mind." Chigs bared his teeth and surged forward with a series of blows that drove Kashatok backward. "Why did Ellam Cua send me on a mission with a female who diverts me from it?"

Kashatok ducked and rolled, surging back to his feet to face Chigs with a raised brow. "Our trickster god isn't always clear. Perhaps your destiny isn't as straightforward as you thought."

Chigs lowered his staff, frowning. "What are you saying?"

"Don't throw away a chance at happiness because you think it's not part of some grand design." Kashatok clasped his shoulder. "Follow your heart, my friend. That's the only destiny that matters."

The ship's com beeped, and Doug's voice echoed through the room. "I need everyone to meet me in the war room right now."

Kashatok set his staff back in the rack and tilted his head toward the door. "Sounds like we have some women to rescue."

Chigs put his staff away and trudged down the hall, stewing over the choices in front of him. He knew what his heart wanted, but could he really choose between love and duty? He'd once gone to Emmy for advice. Perhaps it was time to speak with her again. But this time, it wasn't merely advice he'd be asking for.

Chapter Sixteen

After a quick meal with the crew, Emmy excused herself and retreated down the ship's silent corridors to her office. Chigs hadn't come to the mess hall to eat, and she was certain he must be avoiding her. *Can you blame him?* After what had happened between them on the shuttle, she doubted they'd ever feel comfortable in the same room together again.

Sitting at her desk with her eyes closed, she listened to the gentle burble of her meditation fountain, breathing deeply as she tried to regain control of her emotions. *It was nothing more than a fleeting indulgence for us both.* The thought only made her heart ache more. The memory of Chigs's mouth against hers, his hands on her skin, the throbbing line of his cock against her ass permeated her thoughts.

She wanted to blame him for everything, but couldn't. She'd invited his kiss, despite knowing that Chigs's heart could never truly belong to her. He'd acted on it, but she shared responsibility for the tangled web they'd woven together. Frustration and guilt created a maelstrom in the pit of her stomach.

Unable to find peace, she exhaled slowly and opened her eyes. Her gaze fell on the box Rust had given her when she'd stepped off the shuttle. Inside was her toy dragon, the one he'd ripped apart during their last session, now repaired. If only everything could be fixed so easily.

"Em, are you okay?"

Emmy's head jerked toward the doorway. Marlis stood there, blonde brows knit in concern. Emmy tried to smile reassuringly. "Tired is all. It was a long mission."

Marlis sauntered in and propped a hip on the edge of Emmy's desk. "So, how'd things go with Dafari?"

Emmy blinked. This entire thing with Dafari had been such a big deal a few days ago, but now she hardly gave him a passing thought. "It was nothing, really."

"Mm." Marlis cocked her head. "Then what's got you so down?"

"Me? I'm fine," Emmy replied, letting her gaze shift back to the box. "Like I said, just tired."

Marlis nudged the box with her knuckles. "What's in here? I saw Rust give it to you back in the shuttle bay."

Emmy smiled and removed the toy dragon, sitting it on her desk. The stitched repairs to its wings were a little clumsy, but she felt it symbolized the lengths he was willing to go to prove his apology was genuine. "He fixed it for me to make up for a bad counseling session we had."

"Oh, shit. I've heard he can be a bully." Marlis sat up straighter, eyebrows drawn in concern. "You ever need backup, let me know."

Emmy shrugged and smiled. It was nice to have a friend on her side, no matter what. But she didn't want to aggravate anyone against Rust, especially when he appeared to be making progress. "Rust can be gruff, but he's got a good heart."

Marlis's brows relaxed, and a glint entered her gaze. "There something more going on here? A little romance, perhaps?"

Emmy felt her cheeks warm at the suggestion. "Absolutely not."

"Why not? Rust's not bad to look at." Marlis winked suggestively. "If he's got a good heart, he might have other good body parts as well."

Emmy laughed, though her own heart felt heavy. "Marlis, you're incorrigible."

"So I've been told." Marlis laughed.

Her laugh was interrupted by the ship-wide intercom. "I need everyone to meet me in the war room right now," Doug said.

Marlis stood and adjusted her gun belt. "Finally!" she said, striding toward the door. "Been dying for some action."

Emmy felt glued to her chair. Chigs would be there, and she wasn't ready to face him. "I thought Doug would take longer."

"He's a cyborg. They do everything double time." Marlis paused and looked over her shoulder. "You coming?"

"No." Emmy opened a desk drawer and pulled out her data pad, ignoring the thundering pulse in her ears. "I have to catch up on my work."

"Aren't you curious to know what Doug found on that disk?" Marlis eyed her, one brow raised in suspicion.

"My part of the mission is over." Emmy opened a random file on her pad, ignoring Marlis's stare. "You soldier types can handle it from here."

Striding to the desk, Marlis pulled the data pad from Emmy's grasp and towed her to her feet. "Doug called the meeting for everyone, Emmy, and you were part of the fact-finding mission. You have to be there, work or no work."

Emmy sighed in resignation. There was no resisting Marlis when she had her mind set. Chest tight with anxiety, Emmy followed her friend out of the office.

The war room was abuzz with activity when they arrived. A large central table dominated the space, a holographic projector casting complex light patterns above it. Doug stood at the head of the table, while various crew members filled the seats and stood along the walls. Emmy tried to remain inconspicuous, hovering near the back with some of the other crew members, but Doug quickly caught sight of her and gestured her forward.

"Emmy, we saved you a seat." He indicated an empty chair next to Chigs.

Shit. There was no way to gracefully decline, so she moved forward and sat, keeping her weight shifted so she and Chigs didn't bump elbows. He smelled like clean, masculine sweat, and she felt like his merest touch might unravel her. *Keep your focus on Doug,* she told herself. But she felt Chigs staring at her with an intensity that made her prickle with awareness.

"Quiet down," Doug began, his voice commanding the room's attention. "We have a lot to go over and very little time."

The room fell silent as Doug brought up the holographic image of a planet above the center of the table. "I've decrypted the data chip Chigs and Emmy got from their mission. The lab holding the captive women is on a planet called Naraka. It's in a disputed area of Syndicorp space. But the intel also indicates that the lab is in the process of changing location."

Concerned murmurs filled the room.

Tovik slapped a palm against the table. "Then what are we waiting for? Let's go!"

"Slow down, kid," Doug said as the holo image shifted to a set of schematics. "A frontal assault on this place would be suicide—for us and the captured women. But there may be a way to get a team inside to lower the lab's defenses."

"How?" asked Chigs, leaning forward to avidly study the schematics.

Emmy's heart clenched. Of course he was interested. He should be interested. But it felt like she'd just had salt rubbed on a wound.

Doug pointed to a series of symbols on the image. "The orbital patrols could be a problem, but I located an old embassy passcode that will hopefully allow a small shuttle to land."

He continued describing details about the patrol routes while Emmy knotted her fingers together beneath the table, only half listening. These women needed rescuing, but no matter their plight, all she could think about was escaping this meeting. Drowning herself in a vat of chocolate ice cream. Letting the burning behind her eyes resolve into private tears…

The sound of her name brought her back around and she realized everyone in the room was staring at her.

"Okay, Emmy?" Doug said, his cybernetic eye spearing her with green light.

"I'm sorry, I drifted off," Emmy said, cheeks heating. "Can we backtrack a bit?"

Doug frowned, but repeated his summation. "According to the data chip, you're still on the lab's personnel roster. Which means you're the only one who can get us into the building."

Emmy blinked at him. "How the hell am I on the roster?"

"It appears you were never fully removed after you left."

Emmy scowled, bile roiling in her stomach as she realized Dafari must've planned something like this all along. *He left me active as a way to sneak back in.* She swallowed past the growing lump in her throat. "You want me to go on this mission?"

"Yes. Once inside, you and Chigs will make your way to the mainframe and disable the planetary security shields. He's familiar with Syndicorp's base layouts."

"Who else is coming?" Her palms grew sweaty as she thought about being alone with Chigs again.

"The shuttle only carries two, so you two will have to handle the first stage on your own. Once the shields are down, we can land a team near the facility to break the women free and get everyone off planet."

"I see a problem with this plan," said Tovik. "What if there are hybrids there like Rashana? I've been working on a device to block her mind-control powers, but it's still got a lot of bugs."

Emmy's gaze shifted toward Rust, remembering several counseling sessions where he'd talked about the violation he'd felt when Rashana'd tampered with his thoughts. At least Rashana was on their side now, but what if they met more like her? She shuddered at the thought.

"Chigs can use his shielding to protect them both," said Doug. "You can do that, right Chigs?"

Chigs shifted in his chair. "Yes, Emmy's a psychologist, not a soldier. Can't you forge someone else's credentials to take her place?"

Despite her previous hesitation, Chigs's attempt to replace Emmy left her rankled. "I can handle myself, Chigs."

He shot her a look that left her feeling strangely protected and vulnerable at the same time. "I know you can, but you've already risked yourself once for this mission."

"Oooh! Let me pretend to be Emmy!" said Marlis.

Doug shook his head. "The checkpoints inside the facility are genetically linked, and while I might be able to hack a forgery, it would take too much time."

"There will be more women than Emmy to protect once the team is inside," said Rust. "Let me go in Chigs's stead. A cyborg is worth ten regular soldiers."

Chigs bristled. "Says who? I've proven myself in dozens of battles." He rose and placed a hand on the back of Emmy's chair. "And I'll protect my mate with every ounce of my being."

Emmy's heart squeezed at the mention of Chigs's mate, but also raced as she watched Rust flex his cold, metallic arms, each joint clicking with deadly precision.

"You want to prove yourself?" Rust said, baring his teeth. "Let's settle it in the sparring ring."

"You're on." Chigs balled his fists and stepped forward until his thighs hit the edge of the table, his muscles bulging under his skin. Testosterone clogged the air, but nobody seemed to be willing to intervene between the two furious males.

Emmy couldn't take it anymore. She shoved back from the table and drew herself up to her full, if diminutive, height. "Listen to yourselves! While you're arguing, innocent women could be suffering and dying."

All eyes turned to her. Rust continued scowling, but lowered his arms to his sides. Chigs turned to face her, palms up as if to placate her. Doug's usually passive features seemed to hold a smirk, and Marlis nudged her with an elbow. "Go get 'em, Em."

Taking a deep breath, Emmy pointed toward the door. "While you to wrap up your bickering, I'm going to go prepare for this mission. I'll be at the shuttle waiting."

With that, Emmy wheeled around and strode from the room, knowing Chigs would win out in the end. They were going to rescue his mate. *And then I can move past this heartbreak for good.*

Chapter Seventeen

Chigs sat hunched over the antiquated shuttle controls, his large hands dwarfing the joystick as he navigated away from the *Icarus*. Although Tovik had given the shuttle a quick once-over, the control console flickered with unreliable luminescence.

Emmy sat silently in the co-pilot seat, gaze doggedly locked on the forward viewscreen. She'd barely spoken five words since he'd joined her in the shuttle bay to begin the mission.

The decision for him to accompany Emmy to Naraka had been a foregone conclusion, one even Rust didn't argue after witnessing Emmy's outburst. Yet Chigs felt awkwardly embarrassed. He was usually focused and decisive, but the new emotions he felt around Emmy left him unbalanced.

He cast a sidelong glance at her, the dim light of distant stars from the viewscreen etching the silver piping on her Syndicorp uniform. Clearing his throat, he said, "Sure is lucky Doug got us this undocumented shuttle on Jarboa, huh?"

She shrugged and nodded, eyes not leaving the screen.

Uminaq. She wasn't making this easy. He was dying to confess his change of heart. But how do you tell a woman who's been hurt by love that she's your chosen one, especially when she thinks she's just helping you rescue another?

He licked his lips and tried again. "Once we get inside, how long do you think it'll take to reach the mainframe?"

"Depends on how many guards we meet," she clipped out. "My clearance is for the patient levels, not security."

Reminded of the danger he was putting her in, Chigs clenched his teeth, chastising himself for even considering this as the appropriate moment to bare his soul. Planning for this mission and Emmy's safety should be at the top of his thoughts. "I'm hoping you can sweet talk our way out of any confrontations, but I can take out a few guards if necessary."

"Let's hope it's not." She looked at him for the first time since he'd joined her on the shuttle. "There will also be cameras everywhere. You brought your disguise?"

Chigs nodded, tapping the holo projector around his throat. "Tovik added a Syndicorp uniform to my wardrobe."

She nodded curtly and returned her attention to the viewscreen. "Good."

He sighed, the sound lost amidst the low drone of the shuttle's engines, yearning for the easy companionship they'd shared during their time on Alleigh. *Just say it.* He cleared his throat again. "Emmy, I want to talk to you about what happened between us."

Her hands curled into fists on her lap, and she shook her head. "I'm not in the mood to talk, Chigs. Let's just focus on getting through this alive, okay? We can't afford distractions."

"Sure," he muttered, knowing she was right. Much as he wanted to get this weight off his chest, he focused on the controls. His confession would have to wait. For now, he steered their fragile vessel onward, toward the growing circle of light that was the planet Naraka.

Soon it loomed large in the viewscreen, an expanse of tan and black with dust clouds swirling across the surface. The shuttle creaked as they entered the outer stratosphere, and the yoke vibrated under Chigs's palms.

"Shuttle AX-237, this is Naraka Orbital Patrol," crackled a voice over the comm. "You've entered restricted airspace. Please leave the area immediately."

"We have clearance," Chigs replied. He punched in the passcode Doug had provided, stomach churning like the dust clouds below.

"Processing," came the terse reply.

Chigs gripped the yoke with sweaty palms. If the code didn't work, the best they could hope for was being ordered to turn around. But there was also a chance they'd be blown to space dust.

Silence stretched like a wire about to snap. In the darkness beyond the planet's curved surface, the hailing patrol ship drifted into view like a predator lying in wait.

Finally, the voice over the comm said, "Your clearance code is expired."

Breathing shallowly, Chigs tightened his grip on the joystick, wishing it was the control for a gun turret. At least then he had a fighting chance against the other ship. He glanced at Emmy's pale face. "Buckle in. This could get ugly."

"Wait." She leaned forward and engaged the comm. "This is Dr. Emilia Voss, here to oversee the transport of test subjects. Let us land and I'll get this cleared up." She then rattled off credentials and additional authorization codes with such rapid confidence that even Chigs almost believed she still worked for the lab.

"Can't let you land without the proper clearance," the patrol insisted.

"Unless you want to face the director's ire, I suggest you check my credentials and let me through," Emmy said. "This is a time-sensitive mission, and any delay could compromise years of research."

Another moment of silence passed, then the voice said, "Dr. Voss, your status has been confirmed. Please be sure to update your ship's passcode for future entries. Be advised, a severe dust storm is active on the surface. Proceed with caution."

"Understood," Emmy replied coolly, then cut the link.

As the patrol ship peeled away, Chigs gave her an appreciative glance. "Nicely done."

Emmy blew out a loud breath. "I'm not sure my story will hold up if he asks around. Let's get down there before he digs any deeper."

He aimed the shuttle toward the surface. The hull rattled, drowning out the static-filled hum of the console. Chigs adjusted the throttle, trying to stabilize their course. "He wasn't kidding about that storm. Better buckle in."

Though the inertial dampeners should keep them safely seated for the ride down, he was wary of this beat up old shuttle.

Emmy struggled to pull her harness across her body. He longed to reach across to assist her, to take her shaking hand in his, but focused on keeping his grip on the juddering yoke.

As they pierced the hazy veil of the storm, trails of black dust clouds snaked over the viewscreen. The small craft convulsed and pitched sideways. Emmy gasped and gripped her armrests while Chigs engaged his ionic shielding, securing himself in place. He wished he could provide Emmy the same measure of safety.

The shuttle bucked and shivered, while the ship's metal hull groaned with the sound of stressed metal. A vibration started in the floor panels, a treacherous shiver that traveled up through Chigs's boots and settled like ice in his veins.

"Steady, girl," he murmured to the shuttle, though it was his own nerves he sought to calm. He had flown basic missions, but piloting was not his calling. Ellam Cua had shaped him for battle, not finesse with thrusters and trajectory calculations. Through the viewscreen, he caught glimpses of craggy rock and drifting sand through brief openings in the storm.

A jolt sent the shuttle spiraling, the rasp of blowing sand on metal nearly deafening. He realized the inertial dampeners were offline when a stray ration pack floated past him toward the viewscreen. The pack wobbled uncertainly for a few heartbeats, then dropped like a stone as the dampeners came back online.

He glanced at Emmy, who sat gripping her armrests, face pale. "Hang in there," he said. "Almost there."

But they weren't. The readings on his control panel said they were off course. He jerked hard on the yoke, trying to steer them back toward the facility's landing pad. But he couldn't get the gyros to compensate, sending the shuttle back into a spin.

Suddenly, a wrenching pop filled the cabin, like a cable snapping under too much tension. To his horror, the co-pilot chair ripped free, slamming the top of Emmy's headrest into the ceiling. She screamed, raising her arms to protect her face as the ceiling panel broke free, spilling cables and wires down around her. Then Emmy and the entire chair sailed backward, out of sight.

A glance over his shoulder showed her seat wedged sideways against the wall near the door. He couldn't see her face to know if she was all right. "Emmy!" he shouted, voice lost amidst a cacophony of alarms and the banshee wail of the storm outside.

The yoke jerked in his hands again, and he whipped his attention back to the controls. The shuttle felt like it was about to be ripped apart, and his altimeter showed the ground quickly approaching. He had to focus, or they'd be splatted like insects. *Ellam Cua, please help...*

The swirl of dust outside the viewscreen was now a solid wall as Chigs wrestled with the controls, fighting for mastery over the careening shuttle. His sensors were going haywire, confused by the density of blowing sand. All Chigs could do was hold on, navigating by instinct and his desperate, silent prayers to Ellam Cua.

With a bone-jarring crash, they hit the surface, metal screeching as the shuttle carved a jagged furrow through the landscape. The acrid tang of fried circuits filled the air, a billowing cloud of smoke from the control panel stinging Chigs's nostrils.

Jumping to his feet, he stumbled through the haze toward Emmy. She was still strapped to her chair, the jagged metal that had once held it to the deck now embedded in the access panel of the thruster control unit. More smoke curled from the damaged panel like ghostly fingers, and sparking wires swayed alarmingly close to Emmy's head. Her eyes were closed, but she appeared to be unharmed.

He dropped to his knees beside her, hands trembling as he jerked at the release of her seat harness. She slumped limp into his arms when the restraint finally let go.

"Emmy! Emmy, wake up!" he cried, shaking her gently.

She didn't move.

"No, no, no," Chigs muttered, panic clawing up his throat. His fingers sought the pulse at her neck. The beat under his fingertips was weak but steady, a symphony amidst chaos. Relief shuddered through him when her eyelids fluttered.

"Stay with me, Emmy," he said, the smoky air making his voice raspy. They had to get out of the shuttle before the smoke suffocated them.

"Chigs?" Her voice was faint.

"Right here," he assured her, cradling her against his chest as he stood.

"Did we... make it?" she slurred.

"We're alive, and that's what matters. We need to find shelter."

He activated his ionic shielding, a shimmering bubble enveloping them both, then kicked open the hatch. Sand blasted against the shield, an abrasive roar that took every ounce of his concentration to keep at bay. He stepped out into the storm, setting a course for the shadowy outline of the nearest rock formation, praying it might offer some respite.

Emmy's arms tightened around his neck, and she pressed her cheek against his chest. With each plodding step, he became more aware of not just her physical presence, but the emotional gravity she'd come to hold in his life. *I could've lost her.*

The thought of existing without Emmy was unbearable.

When they reached the rocks, Chigs carefully laid her down on the soft sand, his heart pounding with both fear and relief. The rocks created a sanctuary of sorts, an area where the racing sands couldn't reach them. Though the sandstorm still howled like a vicious animal, at least Chigs could drop his shielding for a little while.

"Are you okay?" he asked, gently pushing her thick brown hair off her forehead to reveal a bruise.

"I think so." She sat up and took stock of herself, wincing when her fingers touched the bruise. "Just a little knocked around."

All the fear and desperation Chigs'd felt during their descent cracked open like a dam. He placed both hands on her shoulders, drawing her attention to his face. "Emmy, I need to tell you something. My mate isn't in that lab."

She frowned. "Wh-what do you mean? Did you have another dream?"

"No. I just... I think I was wrong. Emmy, I believe you are my mate."

Chapter Eighteen

Emmy sat with her back against the rough stone of their shelter, its jagged edges sharp through the fabric of her uniform. The wind howled across the narrow opening in the rock, hot and gritty, the curtain of driving sand trapping them inside. A storm of equal proportion raged inside Emmy's mind. Chigs's confession was more disorienting than the crash had been.

He thinks I'm his mate?

She couldn't deny that her heart yearned to accept his love. Yet fear whispered insidious doubts. She'd been burned by Dafari's betrayal, then razed again by Mek's obliviousness. Each wound had calloused her heart a little more.

As a psychologist, she was trained to compartmentalize and view her patients' situations objectively. Yet here she was, drowning in a tumultuous sea of her own vulnerability. If someone came to her with a similar dilemma, what advice would she give?

"Emmy, did you hear what I said?" Chigs's voice sounded strained. He looked disheveled from the storm, his dark hair a wild mess. Sand clung to his beard. Was he another emotional time bomb waiting to detonate? Or could he be the partner she'd always longed for, someone she could trust implicitly?

Emmy licked her lips, tasting grit. Her heart yearned for this gorgeous, honorable male kneeling before her now, sincerity burning in his copper eyes.

But her mind screamed for self-preservation. *Don't be fooled again! You trusted before and look what it cost you.*

She exhaled a shaky breath, tugging at her cloak of professional objectivity. "I heard you, yes. But I'm afraid this is just you reacting to stress."

"No, it's not, Emmy. I can't stop thinking about you." His copper gaze didn't waver.

At least it was gratifying to know she hadn't been alone in her obsession, but that didn't mean they were mates for life. He was most likely experiencing a classic case of cold feet now that they were so near his goal of finding the denaidan women where his true future—and mate—lay.

Emmy chewed her bottom lip, trying to see things from outside her own emotions. "I think your feelings are probably arising from transference," she said.

His eyes narrowed. "What's transference?"

"It's a common phenomenon between doctors and their patients. It's when feelings about someone in your past are subconsciously projected onto your therapist." She spoke with all the zeal of a first-year psychology student, despite the denial in her heart. "But the emotions aren't real."

"First of all, you're not my therapist," Chigs pointed out. "Second, I know now that my dream was guiding me to *you* all along." He chuckled dryly and shook his head. "Ellam Cua is probably laughing right now over my misinterpretation. I want to save these denaidan women, but the actual goal Ellam Cua intended me to reach was you."

Emmy swallowed, trying to suppress the flutter in her stomach, the ache in her chest. *He thinks the dream was about me.* Past betrayals played again through her consciousness. She wanted Chigs far more than she'd ever wanted any of them. Yet how could she trust herself to recognize love now when it had betrayed her so cruelly before?

"I want to believe you, Chigs. More than anything." She shook her head. "But I can't. Not after what I went through with Dafari and other lovers."

Chigs reached out, engulfing her small hands in his larger, calloused ones. "I'm not them, Emmy. What we have is real, tangible. This isn't some scientific mumbo-jumbo. It isn't a fleeting infatuation or lustful diversion. I will never choose another, even if you reject me." His thumb stroked over her knuckles in a soothing caress that sent shivers right to her core. "You are my destiny."

Emmy suddenly realized she was being a coward. She'd come to trust Chigs deeply, and knew, without a shred of doubt, that he would never intentionally hurt her. His loyalty, his unflinching integrity—those qualities had captivated her as surely as his striking eyes and powerful physique. He was worthy of her trust, of her heart, if she could find the courage.

Releasing her hands, Chigs stood, his broad frame stooped beneath the low rock ceiling. "But if you don't feel the same, I won't pressure you. Just know that I'll be waiting. Always."

His offer of space felt like a stopper had just been pulled from the bottle of her emotions, dissipating the storm within her. She glanced at the curtain of sand, realizing how close they'd come to death in that crash. She didn't want to die, never knowing what it was to be truly loved.

Before he could move away, Emmy reached up and took his hand again. "Wait." Her voice caught on the lump in her throat, but she found the courage to push past it. "I think… I want to take that chance. On us."

Chigs was motionless for a handful of heartbeats, his fingers curled around hers. Then, with a low rumbling growl, he swept her up into his arms and captured her lips in a searing kiss. Emmy gasped at the ferocity of his embrace, instinctively opening for the questing stroke of his tongue. She clung to his shoulders, fingers tangling in the long hair at the nape of his neck as her desire burst into flames.

His large hands roamed over her body with possessive urgency, calloused pads leaving trails of delicious friction through the thin fabric of her shirt. When his fingers found the soft swell of her breast, she arched into his touch with a ragged gasp.

Panting harshly, Chigs murmured against her tingling lips, "You are my *unqu akhala,* my heart's choice."

Emmy's hands trembled as she traced her fingers through the rough beard covering his jaw. "Yes," she whispered fervently. "Yours."

They kissed passionately until they were both left panting. Her hands struggled with the fastening on the front of his uniform, palms sliding under the fabric against his skin.

"Let me see you, *akhala*." He helped her shrug out of her uniform shirt and bra, his gaze devouring every newly exposed inch of flushed skin. Emmy felt powerful and cherished.

He nuzzled the slender column of her neck, his deft fingers plucking at her nipples until they peaked into aching points. Heat bloomed in Emmy's core, and she rocked her hips against his solid length, seeking friction, craving that intimate connection. "Chigs, please..."

He growled against the throbbing pulse at her throat. "Patience, *akhala*. Let me worship you properly first."

Removing his shirt, he laid it on the soft sand like a blanket in the middle of the cave before lowering her onto it and resuming his attention.

His lips trailed lower, nibbling her collarbone before blazing a molten path between the valley of her breasts. When he closed his mouth over one tight peak, Emmy cried out, voice lost to the storm as warm wet heat pulsed between her thighs.

She slid her hand down the hard planes of his chest, seeking the stiff rod of his arousal where it pressed along her hip. He felt enormous, straining against his pants, long and hard. She fumbled at the closure of his waistband, but he pulled away, tugging her pants and panties off in what felt like one deft sweep of his arm. His palms were like brands against her skin as he knelt between her thighs and pressed them open, pausing only long enough for her to see the glint of passion in his eyes before he delved toward her center.

Her world narrowed to an electric jolt of pleasure as his mouth claimed her sex in a sensual, penetrating kiss. His beard scratched the tender flesh of her inner thighs, adding to the sensation, and she cried out again, bucking upward. He grabbed her ass, holding her against him like he was devouring a feast. The broad swirls of his tongue over her clit alternated with deep penetrating thrusts that brought her to the edge of climax and tumbled her over into ecstasy.

Mindless with bliss, she rode the wave of pleasure, his mouth never stopping until her body stopped convulsing. She floated in a hazy, lust-soaked delirium, half conscious of Chigs shedding his pants before climbing on top of her, one heavy thigh pressed against the slickness between her legs. The hot, thick line of his cock rested against her hip bone, pulsing as if in time to a heartbeat.

He leaned close to her ear, his breath hot against her skin. "Last chance to change your mind, *akhala*. There will be no turning back after this."

Her fingers curled into the soft sand as she opened her eyes to lock gazes with him, his heavy-lidded eyes dark with passion. "I want you, Chigs."

Satisfaction lit his features, and he shifted, placing the broad head of his member against her opening. She was slick and ready, widening her legs to accept him. With excruciating purpose, he pushed into her, stretching her until she was panting with a pleasure that verged on pain. She clawed his back, needing him more than she'd ever needed anyone or anything in her entire existence.

"Chigs, please…" She wrapped her ankles around his hard backside and pulled him deep inside her, gasping as his hips settled against hers and his cock filled her completely.

He groaned. "My Emmy."

Kissing her with an urgent passion, he began to rock, stroking in and out in an increasing rhythm that made her insides flutter and an orgasm rise within her once again. Over and over, he drove into her, his huge body covering hers. All she could do was try not to drown as a tsunami of sensation carried her up, up, up, then rolled her over in a wave of pleasure. She thought she might never touch the ground again.

With a shudder, Chigs thrust forward a final time, filling her with the heat of his release.

She clung to his waist as her orgasm responded to his, an echo of micro shocks that went beyond mere carnal compulsions. It was as if their souls were joining. As if the entire purpose of the universe had come down to a single moment.

Chigs rolled to the side to take his weight off of her, propping his head on his elbow to look into her face. "I love you, Emmy. You're my destiny, my chosen."

A profound sense of peace and rightness settled over Emmy. This was her path, her destiny—not chosen for her by the capricious hand of fate, but claimed through her own courage and open heart. "And you are mine, Chigs."

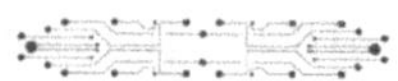

Emmy woke to find Chigs gone. His shirt still spread against the sandy ground beneath her, her clothes draped like blankets across her body. Sitting up, she glanced around, peering through the darkness. The air had cooled with the coming of night. "Chigs?" Her voice echoed hollowly from the cavern walls.

The wind outside had eased, and the narrow opening in the rock gave her a glimpse of a velvet black sky glistening with stars. Rising, she quickly dressed, fumbling with the closures on her uniform. Surely he hadn't left her here alone? She went to the cave entrance and looked outside. Tiny stings of blowing sand pricked her skin, but at least it wasn't trying to flay her alive.

"Chigs!" She moved forward.

Within two steps, she was wading halfway up to her shins in sand. She cartwheeled her arms, but fell backward onto her ass. Crawling back inside the shelter, she rubbed the grit from her eyes.

What was Chigs up to? She couldn't imagine why he'd left her here to go off on his own. What if he got lost in the desert? Panicked questions zipped through her mind one after another as she imagined herself stranded in this desolate wasteland alone.

Heart pounding against her ribs, she paced back and forth in the cramped shelter, watching the entrance. He'd be back soon, right? The minutes stretched into an eternity as she waited. Just as she was considering heading back out to look for him, Chigs appeared with a pack slung over one shoulder.

"Where did you go? I was worried sick!"

"Sorry, *akhala*. I didn't mean to scare you." He stepped inside, black sand pouring from his broad shoulders like rain. "I went to check on the shuttle."

"Is it fixable?"

"Not by me," he said with a grimace. "The wiring's fried."

She returned his pained expression. "Any idea how far we are from the lab?"

He pulled a small device from the pack and peered at the screen. "Looks like the facility is only a few clicks away. It should take a couple of hours to reach it on foot."

She thought about the way the desert had tried to swallow her like quicksand. "On foot? How do we keep from sinking?"

"I'll carry you using my ionic powers." He hooked the scanner on his belt before retrieving a unit of water from the pack and handing it to her. "At least Tovik packed us a few supplies, though I have a few choice words for him about his shuttle maintenance skills when we get back to the Icarus."

"I'm sure the lab's security team knows we crashed." She popped the seal on the water and took a deep gulp, realizing how parched her throat was. She wanted to down the entire thing but wasn't sure how much water they had available, so she handed it back to Chigs instead. "Should we wait for a search party?"

Chigs took a small sip of water before capping it and putting it away. So she'd been right—that was probably the only source of water they had. "We weren't exactly on the guest list. Might be better if we get to the lab on our own."

She grimaced, remembering their plan to bluff their way in. Arriving on foot would only add to the scrutiny. "They probably don't have many guests knock at their front door, either."

"Every facility I was ever stationed at during my Syndicorp days had a back door. The layouts are always similar. I'm sure I can find it."

Emmy nodded, remembering rumors of an executive escape tunnel back on Xeranis. That way, the bigwigs wouldn't be trapped if the convicts rioted. "If you think so."

"Ellam Cua will guide us. Assuming I don't misinterpret the signs again." His teeth flashed in a wry grin in the darkness. "Better get going." He crouched down with his back to her. "Hop on."

Placing one hand on his shoulder for balance, Emmy climbed onto his back. The subtle scents of earth and masculine sweat clung to him, and her nipples tightened with awareness as they pressed against his muscular shoulder blades. She leaned close to his ear. "Is it wrong I want you again?"

He craned his neck around to meet her gaze, his eyes glinting in the darkness. "Don't tempt me, *akhala*."

She smiled, settling herself more comfortably against him. They might be on a dangerous mission, but she didn't think she'd ever felt so happy in her life.

CHAPTER NINETEEN

Chigs's feet shushed over the sand, kept from sinking by his ionic powers. Every inch of his skin felt alive, sensitive to Emmy's reassuring weight on his back, her breath warming his neck as he moved. He hadn't been able to stop grinning since he'd felt the mate bond settle into place.

Emmy is mine. His entire soul sang with elation.

To think she'd been with the rebellion for nearly a year, right in front of him almost every day, and he'd been too blind to notice the perfection so close at hand. *No wonder Ellam Cua tormented me with that damnable dream.*

Emmy adjusted her grip on him, her soft, feminine scent like a drug in the dusty air.

"Doing okay?" he asked. The edge of a pale pink moon had just crested the horizon, outlining the forms of towering beige rocks that jutted into an obsidian sky.

"Yes," Emmy said, adjusting her hold. "Am I too heavy? Do you need to rest?"

He chuckled. "Not at all. I barely know you're there." Which wasn't quite true, not when his every thought was about her. But now wasn't the time to be thinking about getting her naked again. "How's our progress?" he asked, pulling the scanner from his belt and handing it to her.

She took it, propping it on his shoulder to look at it as he continued walking. "I think we need to head left a bit more."

He adjusted course and trekked on, aiming toward a cluster of rocks in the distance.

"Does it look like those rocks are moving?" Emmy asked, her fingers digging into his shoulders.

He paused, realizing the rocks were indeed wavering like a mirage in the night air. The ground beneath his feet rumbled like the purr of a well-tuned burn drive. This wasn't good.

"What's happening?" Emmy whispered, voice barely audible. But he felt her terror vibrating along their mate bond as if it was his own.

Chigs peered into the darkness, trying to discern the source of the sound. He released one of Emmy's legs and reached for the gun at his hip just as the ground beneath them erupted. He arced through the air, landing hard on the sand before the surface tension gave way like water beneath him. Emmy's weight had vanished.

A shadow blocked the moon's light as a colossal beast with what looked like hundreds of tiny legs rose from the sand. Its body gleamed amethyst in the pale moonlight, hardened by what looked like overlapping plates of metal or chiton.

He'd managed to keep hold of his gun, but it suddenly felt woefully inadequate.

Pulse racing, he scrambled upright and scanned the area for Emmy as the sand bucked and rolled under his feet. He spotted her half-buried in the sand on the other side of the creature, floundering like a drowning woman in its wake.

"Emmy, I'm coming!" The deafening sound of its tunneling filled the air as he leaped past the creature's undulating body. Even with his ionic shielding engaged, the churning sand threatened to swallow him whole.

Emmy's head dipped out of sight, only to rise again a few meters away. Arms flailing, she futilely clawed at the shifting surface. "Chigs!"

The creature drilled forward with relentless speed. Its length seemed to stretch forever, throwing a choking cloud of sand into the air with its many legs.

With a surge of adrenaline, Chigs launched himself up and over the beast's back, landing on the rolling sand and focusing all his energy into his feet to keep himself from sinking. Grasping one of Emmy's arms, he pulled her free of the sucking maelstrom and bolted for some nearby boulders.

The rumbling continued behind him, and he didn't stop running until they were on solid ground. Finally, he paused to catch his breath.

Emmy clung to him, coughing up sand. "What the hell was that thing?"

"No clue," he said, mouth dry with grit. "But at least it isn't chasing us."

They both gazed back at the creature, now fading into the distance, its trail marked by a haze of dust.

Chigs turned back to Emmy, running his hands down her arms and hips to reassure himself she was unharmed. "Are you okay? I thought I'd lost you for a moment."

"Yeah, me too." She hugged him tightly. "I'm okay, though. Thanks for saving me."

"I'll never let anything happen to you," he promised, though fear still rattled his bones. He couldn't wait for this mission to be over. "Let's keep moving. Which direction do we go?"

With a grimace, Emmy looked down at her hands. "I don't know. I lost the scanner."

"*Uminaq.*" Then, realizing the curse might've come across as a reprimand, he added, "Don't worry, we'll find the base without it." He looked around, hoping for some sign of the base on the monotonous landscape.

Emmy pointed at the horizon. "I think we were heading toward that cluster of stars. The one shaped like a crescent."

He smiled at her, glad she'd been paying attention, since he'd apparently been too caught up in thinking about their mate bond. "Great."

She clambered onto his back, and he once more continued their journey. As the pale purple light of pre-dawn filled the sky, he spotted a metallic glint among a cluster of stones in the distance. "I think I see something," he said

Emmy rested her chin on his shoulder. "The rocks?"

"Syndicorp likes to hide their bases underground," he said. "That's probably the entrance to the shuttle bay we're seeing."

"How do we find the back door?"

"Once we're closer, we'll circle around. I can use my ionic senses to detect the electromagnetic signature on the lock."

He picked up his pace, relieved when they visually confirmed a pair of massive cargo bay doors hidden under a broad overhang of stone. Giving the doors a wide berth, they circled around to the back of the rock formation. The sand was firmer next to the boulders. He let Emmy slide down his back, though she still sank up past her ankles. The desert's nighttime chill seeped through his clothes.

"I can't maintain my shield and focus on finding the lock at the same time," he told her. "Stay here while I look for the door."

"No way." Arms crossed over her chest to ward off the chill, Emmy glanced toward the expanse of desert.

"What if another monster appears? I'll crawl behind you if I have to, but we're sticking together."

He opened his mouth to argue, but thought better of it. He didn't like the idea of her being left behind, either. "All right."

Dropping to the ground, he began to half-swim, half-crawl on his belly like a snake across the powdery surface. Every few meters, he paused to search the area with his ionic senses, seeking a faint tingle to alert him of nearby electronics.

Emmy lagged behind, white clouds of fog a sign of her labored breathing. Though it was cold now, the sun would rise all too soon, and the heat would be unbearable. He had to find the back door quickly.

As he faced ahead once more, a small golden creature with ten legs darted across the dark sand in front of him. Chigs tensed, wary of another dangerous encounter. The animal scaled the nearby rock wall and disappeared somewhere overhead. As Chigs followed its upward path, he felt the familiar pulsing prickle of an electromagnetic field.

Standing, he spotted a telltale indentation in the stone about an arm's length above his head. Using his ionic power, he jumped and pulled himself up onto a ledge that led to a shallow cave. A biometric security panel glowed on the far wall. "Praise Ellam Cua," he murmured.

He released a wave of ionic energy that should scramble any active surveillance equipment, then jumped down and hurried to help Emmy.

When they were safely inside the cave, she leaned against a wall, panting hard. Black sand caked her flushed, sweaty cheeks. She smiled at him. "Nice job."

He smiled back, tucking a stray lock of hair behind her ear. "We should take a minute to clean up before going in."

She grimaced and shook sand from her hair before finger combing it back into a bun. "You mean me. You have your holo projector."

While she brushed more gritty sand from her forehead and cheeks, Chigs activated the device, feeling the familiar tingle as the holographic disguise enveloped him. Like Emmy, he already wore a Syndicorp uniform purloined from one of the lockers on board the *Icarus*, so the projector was only required to hide his copper skin.

Emmy glanced at him and her eyes went wide. "Oh, no..."

"What?"

"Your face…" she gulped. "The projector isn't working."

He looked down at his hands. Patches of his natural copper skin showed through the brown pigment there. His blood felt like it turned to ice as he met her gaze once more. "*Uminaq.* The sand must've rubbed off the paint."

Emmy took a deep breath and pushed her shoulders back. "It'll be okay. Stay here. I'll go find a biohazard suit, or at least a surgical mask. That should cover enough of your features for us to move undetected."

He frowned. "There's no way I'm sending you in there by yourself."

"I have my credentials. I can do this." She clasped his arm briefly. "Trust me."

"Fine. But don't go too far." Checking the settings on his pulse pistols, Chigs ensured they were primed and ready while Emmy pressed her hand against the security panel. A metal hatch embedded in the stone floor released with a soft click and the hiss of falling sand.

Praying there were no guards stationed inside, he lifted the hatch the rest of the way, releasing a gust of musty air, as if it had been trapped inside for far too long. A metal ladder descended into a corridor lit by a single yellow emergency light. The rest of the hall waited in darkness. *Is the base abandoned?* His heart squeezed.

Emmy voiced his concern before he could. "What if we're too late and they've already moved the lab?"

Even as she said it, a faint noise reached his ears, the distant echo of laughter followed by a quick fade of voices.

"Someone's here," Chigs whispered. "We're not too late."

With a quick nod, Emmy swung her feet over the edge and started down. The clang of her boots on the metal rungs seemed overly loud in the silence. At the bottom, she looked up. "I'll be back soon." He barely caught the reflection of her teeth as she gave him one last grin.

Then she disappeared into the darkness.

Chapter Twenty

Emmy brushed a bead of sweat from her brow and cautiously advanced down the deserted hallway, pulse pounding in her ears. She'd put on an air of confidence with Chigs when she'd insisted she go alone to find something to disguise him, but in truth, she was terrified. What if she bumped into an old colleague? What if someone questioned her credentials? Would something like a surgical mask be enough to disguise Chigs's copper skin and full beard, or was this entire mission doomed to fail before it even began?

Failure isn't an option. Not only did the denaidan women's lives hang in the balance, but she and Chigs no longer had a shuttle. They couldn't leave. The only recourse was to hack the security protocols so the rest of their crew could land. The weight of the situation loomed above her like an impending avalanche.

She peeked around the dark corner at the end of a hall to find an alcove and another door. On the wall nearby, a security panel glowed with blue light.

"Shit," she murmured, the taste of worry sharp on her tongue. She hadn't expected another door so quickly. What if there were guards stationed on the other side?

She took a deep breath and let it out slowly. *It's going to be okay. If I encounter guards, I'll just tell them my shuttle crashed, and this was the closest door.*

Gathering her courage, she entered the alcove and placed a shaky hand against the sensor.

A blinking cursor appeared, requesting a security code. Panic fluttered in her chest like a trapped bird. She hadn't needed a security code to open the outer door, only her palm print. Perhaps her credentials would work? She began entering her employee ID, but after the first five symbols, a harsh beep sounded, and the panel began flashing red.

She flinched back in panic, staring at her own red-tinged reflection on the metal door. After a few moments, the panel turned blue again. *Thank heavens.* It seemed no one had been alerted to her mistake.

She rubbed her sweaty palm against her thigh. Obviously, her employee number wasn't the way in. *Maybe I missed something during Doug's meeting.* To be fair, her thoughts really hadn't been focused on the discussion. Abandoning the security panel, she retraced her steps back to Chigs.

The moment her foot touched the bottom rung of the ladder, Chigs reached down through the hatch and pulled her up into his arms. "That was fast." He glanced at her empty hands. "No mask?"

"There's another locked door around the corner, and my credentials won't open it." She raised her eyebrows hopefully. "Did Doug mention a password?"

Chigs shook his head. "No. He just said you're on the roster and your biometrics could get us through security."

"What should we do now?"

"I'll get it open." He jumped down through the hatch into the corridor beside her, forgoing the ladder completely.

"Wait!" she whispered, hurrying back down the ladder. His long-legged strides had already carried him to the end of the hall. "If you disable it, you might set off an alarm."

Chigs paused. "You want to try your credentials again?"

Emmy bit her lip, wishing she had an alternative solution. "I guess not."

Nodding resolutely, Chigs placed his hand against the security panel. A barely perceptible ripple of energy laced the air, then the panel went dark. The door slid aside with a subtle hiss of air. Beyond, what appeared to be a dark hallway veered left and right. Faint sounds of activity echoed in the distance, but no alarms.

Breathing shallowly, she lifted her head high, pretending she belonged here before stepping through the doorway. A long, empty corridor stretched in both directions. Widely spaced lights glowed in the ceiling at one end. The other direction disappeared into shadows.

The sound of approaching footsteps echoed through the corridor, and a figure appeared under the lights. Shit.

Chigs was still visible in the open doorway beside her—a door that most likely shouldn't be standing open. "Get out of sight. Someone's coming," she whispered.

With a silent nod, Chigs stepped back.

Thinking it was unlikely she'd been spotted yet in the dark, she stepped back through the door and pressed her hand to the door control to close it. Nothing happened. "Can you close the door?" she hissed at Chigs, voice laced with desperation.

He touched the panel, a look of concentration on his face. "No. My power surge broke it."

The scuff of boot soles on tile now sounded like they were just outside the door. Chigs reached for the pistol at his belt.

Emmy grabbed his arm. If a firefight broke out, it would definitely trigger an alarm.

Recalling all the stories her colleague friends had told her about sneaking off to the custodial closet to make out, she seized Chigs by the lapels of his uniform and pivoted them so his back faced the newcomer. It was a desperate ruse, but she hoped that with Chigs's features hidden in the shadows, they'd appear to be nothing more than a passionate couple seeking solitude. "Play along," she whispered as she sealed her lips to his.

Wrapping his arms around her, Chigs hoisted her with sensual ease, and her legs instinctively wrapped around his waist, securing her against him. The feel of his powerful arms supporting her sent an unexpected thrill of electricity through her system, reminding her of their earlier lovemaking. Chigs must've felt it, too, if the erection pressing through their clothing between her legs was any sign. How insane was it that she was even thinking about having sex right now? At least it would seem real if they were caught.

Unable to hear the footsteps over her own rapid breathing, she cracked open one eye to peer over Chigs's shoulder.

A guard stood there, dark body armor absorbing the dim light cutting in from the open door.

Is he watching us? Perhaps the guard was trying to decide whether to do his duty or allow the lovebirds a moment of peace. She continued kissing Chigs, albeit more stiffly, praying the guard would choose to overlook them and walk on.

Chigs sensed the shift in her mood, his kisses becoming more mechanical. One of his hands slowly left her ass, crawling down her thigh, its movement almost predatory as he reached towards the pistol holstered at his waist.

Still determined to avoid gunfire, Emmy murmured against his lips, "Let me."

Gasping as if she'd just noticed the guard, she unlocked her legs and slid down until her feet touched the floor. Laughing nervously, she stepped around Chigs to face the guard standing a few paces away.

The man's helmet was retracted, his profile bathed in sickly light to reveal a leering expression that made Emmy's skin crawl.

"Just taking a quick break," she said, her voice higher than usual as she adjusted her clothing, acutely aware of her kiss-swollen lips and the pulsing heat between her legs.

The guard's grin broadened, his eyes scanning her up and down with a look that made her want to shower in disinfectant. His attention stopped at her breasts. "This area is off-limits. Though it looks like you aren't."

"Oh…well," she injected a quiver into her voice as if she were truly scared—which, to be fair, wasn't entirely an act. "We were just… we needed some privacy, you know?" Her eyes flickered to Chigs's back, silently urging him to remain still, to trust her just a little longer. "Give us a minute to straighten ourselves and we'll be on our way."

"I should write you up." The man licked his lips. "Though I bet a pretty thing like you probably knows how to persuade me to forget I saw anything."

Her stomach churned, and she opened her mouth to reply, but before she could utter a sound, Chigs slammed into the guard with the ferocity of a lightning bolt. The air rippled with a burst of ionic energy, and the guard collapsed with a grunt.

"Nobody talks to my mate that way," Chigs ground out, fists clenched as if he was ready to keep fighting.

The guard twitched once, then lay still.

Heart hammering against her ribs, Emmy moved forward to stand next to Chigs. The guard stared lifelessly at the ceiling. "Is he dead?"

"Yeah," Chigs said, kneeling to remove the man's helmet. "There's a weak spot in this model of armor—well, relatively weak, at least to a concentrated ionic pulse. Stopped his heart."

Emmy had never seen a dead body before, let alone witnessed someone being killed. She wasn't sure how to react. Part of her wanted to scream in horror. But another, stronger voice appreciated Chigs for defending her. The guard had been despicable, but that didn't mean he didn't have people who loved him. His family would never know what had happened to him. Never get closure. She couldn't help thinking that she and Chigs could just as easily disappear from existence if things went badly.

She blew out a shaky breath. "Now what do we do?"

Chigs began removing the man's armor. "Give me a minute to put on my new disguise."

Bile rose in Emmy's throat at the thought of donning the clothes of a dead person, but she swallowed it down. At least now they could both enter the lab undetected.

Or so she hoped.

CHAPTER TWENTY-ONE

Chigs took shallow breaths, his chest restrained by the dark mesh of the Syndicorp armor as he and Emmy made their way down another empty hallway. But the tight armor wasn't the only reason he was uncomfortable. Not only was he taking Emmy toward danger, he couldn't help thinking this place felt familiar. How often had he patrolled halls such as these during his time with Syndicorp, never thinking of what might be going on behind closed doors?

Though a murmur of voices sometimes reached them through the ducts overhead, the hallways remained empty. He lagged a few steps behind Emmy, alert to potential enemies at their rear. Hopefully, anyone spotting them on the security cameras wouldn't take a second look at a guard and a researcher taking a stroll together. He could've scrambled the hall cameras with an ionic pulse, but then it would be obvious something was going on.

He gripped the guard's pulse rifle tighter, glaring at yet another door as they approached. His nerves felt like cables about to snap. They'd been leaving the doors alone, minimizing their chance of encountering personnel as they looked for an elevator to reach the mainframe in the basement. Once they'd hacked in to give Doug access to the security systems so a team from the *Icarus* could come back him up, he'd feel much better.

Sounds of muttering voices and beeping medical equipment grew louder as they approached a four-way intersection where signs pointed the way toward Research, Administration, Hospitality, and Security. Emmy glanced at him with uncertainty, and he tilted his head toward Security, knowing guard stations were always located near elevators.

She kept moving, the natural sway of her hips slightly distracting, and Chigs was glad his faceplate hid his gaze as a pair of lab assistants in Syndicorp uniforms exited a doorway to their left. Emmy nodded politely as she passed them, drawing an appreciative glance from one man before he resumed his murmured conversation. Chigs's momentary possessiveness was quickly replaced by approval for his mate, so confident and alluring.

They neared a long observation window, and Emmy's steps faltered as she looked inside. An unfamiliar sensation jabbed him through the connection of their mate bond; regret? She turned her attention straight ahead and continued walking, shoulders now stiff.

He reached the window and peered inside, where several human doctors in Syndicorp uniforms stood around an examination table. The test subject on the table was naked, revealing gleaming copper skin. Chigs's hearts thrummed in his chest. A denaidan female.

His hands ached on the stock of the rifle. How he yearned to blast his way straight through the glass and teach those Syndicorp scum a lesson. Instead, he turned his focus back to Emmy, who was rounding the corner of another intersection. Once the team from the Icarus was on its way, they'd come back for the woman. He hurried on with the taste of bile rising in his throat.

Rounding the corner, he saw a cluster of people emerging from an elevator. They disbursed in either direction, focused on their tasks. Emmy stepped through the elevator doors without even glancing in his direction. *Uminaq.* He'd let himself get too caught up in thoughts of revenge. Protecting Emmy was his priority. He increased his stride, catching the doors with one gloved fist just as they began to slide closed. He stepped inside to find Emmy smiling at a wiry lab tech with ruddy cheeks.

"I haven't seen you around here before," the tech said with a hopeful gleam in his eye. "Which project are you assigned to?"

"Oh, just some cross-departmental assistance," Emmy replied. "For the move."

"Oh, sure, the move." The man looked disappointed. "I'm on the translational genetics team, so I'm stuck here a while longer."

"Translational genetics?" Emmy asked with what sounded like genuine interest. "That sounds fascinating. I'd love to hear more."

"Really?" He beamed. "How about over dinner tonight?"

Emmy toyed with a lock of hair, looking at the man coyly. "Dinner sounds great."

Chigs narrowed his eyes, his grip tightening on the pulse rifle and sweat coating his skin beneath the armor. He knew this was a ruse, but did she have to make it seem so real?

The man's grin broadened, and he thrust a hand toward Emmy. "Wow, okay. My name's Albie."

"Call me Em." She clasped his outstretched hand and leaned closer as if sharing a secret. "Hey, I just got here and have to admit I'm a bit turned around. Can you direct me to the mainframe?"

Why was she asking about the mainframe? Doug already told them it was in the basement. Chigs glanced at the elevator controls and saw that there was no basement level listed. *Oh.* Chigs's appreciation of her strategy ramped up another notch. He'd never have considered asking someone for directions.

"The mainframe?" Albie tilted his head. "Why?"

Emmy rolled her eyes. "The doors in our sector are acting up. Something to do with the security system routing. So frustrating."

"Oh, man, I feel you." Albie rolled his eyes, too. He was still gripping Emmy's hand like a child holding a piece of candy. Chigs was glad his faceplate covered his expression as the man continued, "Especially with so many test subjects out of cryo. I was locked out of the computer for several hours yesterday during active observation."

"That must've been annoying," Emmy said. "How many subjects are you working with?"

"Sixteen. Though it's touch and go with one of them."

"That's too bad," Emmy said, her tone laced with sadness. "So, can you tell me where to find the mainframe?"

"It's in the basement," Albie said. "But the elevator doesn't go all the way down. There's a separate stairwell next to the elevator. Some sort of security measure."

Emmy sighed. "Stairs? Ugh. Why do they have to make everything so hard?"

Albie chuckled. "Tell me about it. But don't worry, I can show you the way."

"Oh, that's so kind of you!" Emmy disentangled her hand from his. "But I don't want to impose on your time."

"Nonsense!" Albie put a hand on Emmy's lower back as if preparing to escort her. "It's no trouble at all. Consider it my small act of rebellion against the higher-ups and their ridiculous floor plans."

Emmy laughed and put a hand on Albie's arm, pulling away gracefully. "I appreciate the offer, Albie, but I'm sure you have important work to attend to. I don't want you to get in trouble with your supervisor."

The doors slid open. Albie scratched the back of his neck, looking at the elevator panel where the button for the lower floor remained lit. "Yeah, I guess you're right."

He stepped partially out of the elevator before turning to look at Emmy one last time. "So, I'll see you in the mess hall at six, then?"

"I look forward to it," Emmy said, giving him a flirty little wave.

Flushing, he backed the rest of the way out, letting the doors slide closed. Emmy released a breath, staring at the doors as the elevator continued downward. "Chigs, I need to get something off my chest."

He nodded, disliking the growing sensation of distance in their mate bond. *She hadn't actually liked that Albie fellow, had she?* "Of course."

She bit her lip, still not looking at him. "That woman we saw, the denaidan… I'm worried you're going to regret bonding with me."

Relief flooded Chigs. "*Anaq!* Don't scare me like that. I thought you were going to tell me you were attracted to that tech."

"Albie?" She gave him a weak smile. "Not my type. But he said there are at least sixteen test subjects here. One of them could be your true mate."

He reached out and stroked her cheek. "You are my *unqu akhala.* Never doubt that, Emmy. I will never regret our bond."

She nodded, but her eyes remained full of doubt. "I suppose we'll see."

Before he could offer more reassurance, the elevator emitted a soft chime, and the doors whooshed open. The time for personal matters would have to wait.

Chigs stepped out first, looking up and down an empty hallway with his ionic senses on high alert. The thrum of what felt like heavy machinery pulsed through the floor against the soles of his boots. He moved forward, seeking the door to the stairwell and found it easily, unguarded and unlocked.

With a quick glance toward Emmy, he opened it and led the way downward. The stairs ended in a long narrow hallway lined with unmarked metal doors, each one flanked by a glowing blue security panel.

"I thought Albie meant there'd be actual security guards," Emmy whispered.

Chigs shrugged. "Maybe he was trying to scare you into thinking you needed him."

Emmy looked around nervously. "Maybe. Which one leads to the mainframe, do you think?"

Moving down the hall, Chigs paused before each door, listening for the telltale thrum of an energy core. He found it at the fifth door, the unmistakable throb like a heartbeat against his ionic senses.

"Here," he said.

Emmy pressed her hand to the door lock. Much to their relief, the door slid open, revealing a tech sitting at a console in the center of the room, staring at security images spread across several monitors. Pale white light flashed like a blinking monster from an immense energy generator in the center of the room.

The tech looked up as Chigs entered. "What—"

Chigs didn't wait for him to finish, rushing forward and breaking his neck with one quick snap. He glanced around the massive room, searching for more Syndicorp personnel. Finding none, he gestured for Emmy to enter.

Emmy stopped just inside the doorway, staring at the dead tech. "Did you really need to kill him? We could've tried making up a story about the malfunctioning doors."

"We can't take chances. Everyone in this facility is a potential threat."

She sighed. "I suppose. But I also remember being one of these people, unaware the project I was working on was causing others harm."

Chigs pressed his lips together, recalling his thoughts from earlier about patrolling halls like these, too. "I understand, but there's too much at stake." He let his gaze roam the various consoles. "Do you have Doug's chip? You need to disable the defense network."

She dug in her pocket and retrieved the chip. "Give me a few minutes."

While she worked on giving Doug access to the security system, Chigs watched the door. His muscles grew more tense with every passing second. If they were caught now, fighting their way out of the basement would be impossible.

"Okay, got it," Emmy said.

Just as the room plunged into blackness.

Chapter Twenty-Two

"Shit," said Emmy, blinking in the darkness. Her fingertips were still poised over the keyboard. She thought she'd entered the commands Doug had given her correctly, but she wasn't a tech specialist. "What the hell did I just do?"

The hum of the power core had ceased, and the whispering air ducts were now still and stagnant, as if holding their breath in anticipation of something sinister. Chigs shuffled in the darkness behind her. "Don't panic. Maybe Doug needed the system to reboot."

As if the computer had heard him, a series of clicking sounds filled the room, and then a low vibration rolled under her feet. The power core returned to life with a dim glow, casting a pale greenish light around them, and her monitor flickered back on.

Relief flooded through her as a message from Doug blinked on the screen. *Override successful. ETA one hour.*

She exhaled in relief. "Looks like he's in."

"Good." Chigs remained focused on the exit. "Let's get back to where we saw that denaidan female and stop their experiment while there's still time."

Emmy's heart clenched, a familiar worry creeping into her thoughts. He'd assured her he loved her, but once he saw a denaidan woman up close, he might change his mind. She pushed the thought away. She'd deal with that later if she had to. Right now, they had someone to save.

"Right." She forced determination into her voice. "Let's go."

Chigs led the way back into the narrow hallway with purposeful strides, his pulse rifle at the ready. Emmy hurried after him, growing sicker with worry as they climbed the stairs and boarded the elevator.

She was staring at their distorted reflections in the metal doors when Chigs startled her from her thoughts. "Are you okay?"

Reluctant to admit she had lingering doubts about what he'd told her earlier, she fidgeted for a moment before coming up with a response. "I was just thinking that I might need a weapon."

He immediately pulled his pulse pistol from its holster and handed it to her. "*Uminaq.* Of course. But if a firefight breaks out, stay behind me. My shield will cover us both."

Emmy accepted the cold weight of the weapon in one hand and took a fortifying breath. The notion they might get into a firefight chased away her romantic worries, and she nodded. This was life or death. She couldn't afford to be distracted by her own wallowing.

The elevator came to a stop, and the doors hissed open. Retracing their steps toward the window where they'd seen the denaidan, the soft echo of their footsteps reverberated off the cold metal walls. It took Emmy a few minutes to realize she no longer heard the murmur of voices or clatter of equipment.

She was about to say something when they reached the observation window where they'd spotted the denaidan woman. Through the glass, she saw that the room now held not one, but many denaidan women wearing what looked like pale blue pajamas sitting together at cafeteria-style tables. The exam table and medical equipment had been pushed to the far wall, and several open doorways provided glimpses of sleeping quarters, giving the impression that this was not a laboratory at all, but a communal living space akin to military barracks.

Emmy frowned, searching for doctors or guards, but saw none. The women moved freely about the room or sat at tables, engaging in quiet conversation or reading data pads. A pair of them played a game of cards. "What's going on?" she whispered. "Why aren't there any guards?"

Face still hidden by his helmet, Chigs muttered, "No idea. But we need to find out what's going on here. Let me go in and talk to them. You stay here and watch our backs."

Nerves jangling with suspicion, she placed her palm against the door control, half expecting it to refuse her access. It slid open with a quiet hiss.

In unison, the women turned to face them. Against their pale blue tunics, their skin glowed like burnished autumn leaves, and the serenity of their gazes reminded her of ancient mythological goddesses.

"By the stars..." Chigs murmured, stepping inside the doorway.

An ache twisted inside Emmy's chest. These women were gorgeous. If it wasn't for the mate bond Chigs had sworn his devotion by, she'd never have been able to compete.

Is the bond even real? She searched her heart for the thread of connection she'd felt during their lovemaking, but couldn't find it. She tried reminding herself that her own worry was probably getting in the way.

Chigs stepped closer to the nearest female. "We're here to free you," he said, his voice full of awe. "Come with us."

Jealousy flared through Emmy, followed by rage that made her fingers itch against the grip of the pistol. Yet as quickly as the feelings had risen, they subsided, replaced by a sudden numbness. She let the hand with the pistol fall slack against her thigh. *Emotional overload.* That must be it. The stress of all this was finally getting to her.

The woman Chigs had addressed stared at him, her eyes cold mirrors reflecting nothing back. "Who are you?"

Chigs removed his helmet, freeing his thick, dark hair and braided beard. "I'm denaidan like you. Here to help you escape."

"Why would we wish to escape?" The women all rose, shuffling to stand together in a group.

Chigs looked over his shoulder at Emmy with a frown. "Are they brainwashed?"

She took in the emotionless stares. Had Dafari's project actually worked? A twisted sense of pride drifted through her. Perhaps all the awful things she'd turned a blind eye to hadn't been in vain. She shook herself, shocked at her own thoughts. "It looks like their personalities may have been altered. The project was supposed to reduce violent tendencies in prisoners."

"How do we reverse it?" he asked.

"They'll need to be reconditioned." Emmy shook her head. "If that's even possible."

Chigs turned back to the women. "Listen to me. Syndicorp destroyed Denaida-daru and took you prisoner. You need to trust me." He moved forward with his hand outstretched in invitation, his voice a blend of command and compassion. "We're here to help you."

One woman stepped forward, placing two fingers against her temple. "We require no assistance." Several others mimicked her action.

The motion struck Emmy as odd, and she frowned. But then her mind settled on one certain thought. *These women are content with their lives.* She moved forward, circling the group so she could see those standing in back. "You want to stay here?"

"Yes." The woman's voice was passive, calming. A voice Emmy would've used to reassure an anxious client. "You should stay, too."

For some inexplicable reason, Emmy found the invitation tempting. She peered between the women toward Chigs. "We can't force them to leave."

Chigs's mouth dropped open in confusion. "What are you saying?"

"If they want to stay and help the project, that's their right."

Scowling, Chigs glared at the woman next to Emmy. Then his eyes widened as if in horror. He lunged forward. "Emmy, come here."

Sudden alarm filled her, and Emmy danced back a few steps, bumping into the table behind her. *Why is he acting so strange?* "Chigs, what's wrong with you?"

"You need to be inside my ionic shield. I need to protect you!" He shoved a woman out of the way, trying to get through.

Several women moved to create a barrier, blocking Emmy's view. But Emmy didn't feel threatened by them. Not by these women. Chigs, on the other hand, was acting a little bit unstable. Emmy glimpsed him bringing his rifle to bear on their group. "I don't want to hurt you, but I will if I have to. Now let her go."

"Chigs, stop!" she cried, trying to push through.

The wall of women refused to budge. Another woman spoke from the crowd, her words soothing and sweet. "We must stay and complete the project. Would you like to help us?"

A sudden yearning filled Emmy for her younger days when her belief in Syndicorp had painted the galaxy in shades of hope. This project was intended to bring peace to the entire universe. Perhaps she'd been wrong to leave it all behind. The only real way to make a difference was here in the lab, not skulking about the galaxy with a ragtag bunch of criminals.

Chigs let out a roar, and Emmy saw one female go flying across the room as three more closed in on either side of her. "Emmy, you have to resist! They're manipulating your mind."

Behind him, the door hissed open, admitting a denaidan woman dressed in a Syndicorp doctor's uniform. She held a data pad and a pair of electronic restraint cuffs. The women surrounding Emmy straightened to attention, their expressions immediately deferential. Four more women held Chigs face down against the floor.

"Dr. Dollard," one of them said. "We have secured the intruders as instructed."

"Take that one to the brig," the newcomer commanded, holding out the cuffs. Then her gaze lasered in on Emmy. "Leave this one to me."

Emmy's conviction wavered as the women holding Chigs bound his hands behind his back with surprising ease. *I need to protect him.* But though her heart raced with the need to act, her body refused to respond to her commands.

The women dragged Chigs from the room, his protests fading to silence as the door slid closed.

The denaidan they'd called Dr. Dollard offered Emmy a hand. "Dr. Voss, I presume? I don't believe we've met. I'm Dr. Dollard."

Emmy frowned. Dollard was supposed to be human and male.

She isn't our enemy. The thought fell over her thoughts like a down blanket. There was something comforting about the doctor's presence, something that made Emmy doubt the chaos that had just unfolded moments ago. Emmy's racing heart calmed. Taking the offered hand, she said, "A pleasure to meet you, doctor. What are you going to do with Chigs?"

A smirk twisted the doctor's perfect copper lips. "He's going to become an important part of our project. Just like you are."

"Me?" Emmy struggled to understand what was happening. Her mate bond with Chigs, her allegiance to the rebels, and her loyalty to Syndicorp all vied for dominance. But her doubts were being slowly smothered by whispered thoughts of reassurance and promise.

"Of course, my dear." The doctor guided her to a seat. "We're delighted you've decided to return to work."

The remaining denaidan women had returned to their previous activities, reading and chatting as if nothing out of the ordinary had happened. As Emmy looked them over, the calm within her settled, as if a fog had lifted in her mind, revealing clarity she hadn't experienced in ages. The persistent ache of guilt and self-doubt melted away, replaced by a serene certainty that this was where she belonged. This was where she could truly make a difference.

Emmy smiled at the doctor. "Thank you, Dr Dollard. I'm really happy to be back."

Chapter Twenty-Three

Emmy couldn't recall how she'd gotten to Dr. Dollard's office, but she knew it was an honor to be invited here. Her gaze drifted from the doctor, who sat across the sleek chrome and black glass desk, to shelves of weighty scientific tomes and twisted, abstract artwork. The walls were adorned with framed holographic images of renowned scientists, each one meticulously lit, giving the office an eerie sense of perfection.

An odd haze clouded her thoughts, skewing her perceptions as if she teetered on the edge of a dream. She shifted in her seat, telling herself the unease slithering through her veins was most likely just nervous excitement over being accepted back into the project.

Dr. Dollard tapped her fingers on the desk's shiny surface, demanding Emmy's attention once more. "You helped build the foundation of our project with your groundbreaking research on emotional transformation, Dr. Voss. Your ability to understand the mind and guide your patients is outstanding. But after your sudden departure, we need to be certain you're ready to come back. Do you understand?"

Oh, yes. My job. Emmy clasped her hands in her lap to control their trembling. *No, not just a job—my life's work.* "Of course, Dr. Dollard. Thank you for offering me a chance to continue with the project."

"Good." Dollard's perfectly sculpted eyebrows furrowed. "Begin by telling me how you and your friend discovered the location of this base."

The urge to divulge everything about the rebel plan was nearly overwhelming. Yet a tiny voice inside her was screaming to resist. "We…" She gulped, her mind in turmoil. *I mustn't talk about the rebels.* And yet, the desire to divulge every scrap of truth to Dr. Dollard was nearly overwhelming.

She settled on a half-truth that lay somewhere in between. "Dr. Dafari sent us to sabotage the project."

"Dafari?" The doctor sneered. "That pathetic excuse for a scientist is behind this?"

Emmy nodded. "He's jealous and angry that he was removed from the project."

Dollard swiped a finger across her desktop and brought up a glowing interface. "I should've guessed he'd cause trouble after my team took over. I suppose I'll have to see that he's retired more permanently."

Alarm rocketed through Emmy's veins. She despised her ex, but he had helped her in the end. He didn't deserve to die. "You don't need to bother. Once the project relocates, he won't be able to find it again."

Turning a shrewd eye back to Emmy, Dollard clucked her tongue. "Don't be naïve, Dr. Voss. The rebels have spies everywhere, even within Syndicorp itself. Surely you know that denaidan you were with is a member of the rebellion?"

Emmy's pulse quickened as the sudden memory of Chigs's face filled her mind. *My mate.* How had she forgotten? He'd been sent to prison. She had to convince Dollard to free him. "Are you sure?"

"He's denaidan—they're all rebels." Dollard tilted her head as if trying to read Emmy's thoughts. "Ah, I see. You've fallen prey to their twisted ideals. Another victim of the baseless propaganda devised by those too narrow-minded to appreciate the gravity of our purpose. I thought you were more intelligent than that, Dr. Voss."

The weight of the fog covering Emmy's mind increased, and she hugged her arms across her chest uncertainly. *Propaganda?* She recalled how she'd been recruited to the rebellion through a RealTime News feed. How she'd felt a vehement desire to join the cause. Was Chigs the noble warrior she imagined him to be? Or were the rebels actually causing more harm than good?

"Why don't you be a smart girl now?" Dr. Dollard continued. "Tell me everything you know about these rebels. Perhaps we can work towards a peaceful resolution that benefits everyone."

The request seemed benign, but paranoia crept up Emmy's spine. Memories of the anger in her friends' voices when they spoke of Syndicorp's atrocities buzzed like an invisible energy shield cloaking her will. *Do not trust this woman.* Yet Emmy felt compelled to say something. "They wanted to rescue the females from the lab."

Dollard sighed. "A perfect example of their misguided purpose. As you saw earlier, the test subjects don't need or want to be saved."

A sense of disorientation washed over Emmy. The denaidan women had refused assistance. She and Chigs had been so sure of their mission, so convinced that they were fighting for the greater good. But now, faced with this unsettling truth, she couldn't help but question everything. "Why don't they want to be free?"

Satisfaction danced in Dollard's eyes. "Did you ever consider that these females might be seeking a better future of their own? They joined the project because they were eager for the chance to transcend their previous limitations."

Emmy's thoughts sharpened as she recalled the prisoners she'd worked with in the early phases of the project. They'd joined the project hoping for an easier sentence. Little had they suspected their futures would be bleak, no matter what they chose. "Were the women actually willing?" Emmy asked, a hint of steel in her voice. "Or coerced?"

Dollard scowled. "The denaidan females were under no duress when they signed their contracts, Dr. Voss. They left their planet willingly."

"Before or after Syndicorp poisoned their world?"

"Before, of course. Syndicorp regrets the unfortunate incident that led to the denaidan people's relocation." Dollard rose and moved around the desk to stand next to Emmy's chair, placing a hand on her shoulder. The weight on Emmy's mind constricted like a vise. "We are not the villains in this narrative. These females were at the mercy of their own physiology long before Syndicorp ever set foot on the planet. We offered them a chance at advancement, a purpose beyond their wildest dreams."

A knot formed in Emmy's stomach as she absorbed Dollard's words. As empaths, the denaidan females had been trapped on their planet, unable to endure the unfiltered emotions of other species. It made sense that some of them may have sought the adventure and escape Syndicorp promised. Perhaps Syndicorp really had been trying to help.

"I... I don't know what to think," Emmy admitted, her voice barely above a whisper. Her thoughts felt as if they were submerged in icy water. No matter how desperately she kicked for the surface, an invisible current pulled her deeper.

"Like you, they want to contribute to the greater good. Your continued work on the project will help make life for these women better than they ever imagined." The pressure of Dollard's hand on her shoulder increased, giving Emmy something to focus on.

She had no reason not to trust Dollard. The doctor was a genius in her field. Emmy's path was directly before her. She just had to submit. Turning to face the doctor's expectant gaze, Emmy couldn't help but feel a sense of pride and excitement at the prospect of pleasing her. "I'll make you proud, Dr. Dollard."

CHAPTER TWENTY-FOUR

The energy field barring the prison door shimmered, painting ghostly lines across Chigs's skin as he paced the length of his cramped cell. *How could I have been so careless?*

The test subjects in the room had all looked fully denaidan, and he'd instinctively raised his empathic shielding to protect them, a practice ingrained in him since youth. Denaidan females were sensitive to emotions, especially from strangers. He'd known they'd be able to sense Emmy's nervous agitation, but figured at least he could protect them from his own.

He'd never considered he might need to protect Emmy from *them*.

I should've anticipated some might be hybrids.

Rashana, the human-denaidan hybrid they'd rescued from one of Dollard's labs, could bend others to her will with nothing but her thoughts. Luckily, Rashana now fought for the rebellion. But these test subjects had been misguided into serving Syndicorp.

Now Emmy was brainwashed, too, being forced to do Ellam Cua knew what against her will. He glared through the energy field toward the control panel across the room on the other side, its glowing blue and yellow lights taunting him. He'd tried using his ionic powers on the barrier, but the electronic restraint cuffs emitted some kind of dampening field that suppressed his abilities.

Chigs threw his bound fists against the invisible barrier, a gesture more out of frustration than any belief it would yield. A numbing jolt raced down his arms and made his hearts hammer fast enough to make him feel sick. Not only was Emmy a prisoner, the team from the *Icarus* was on its way, walking straight into what was likely a trap. If only he could disable these damn cuffs.

With a hiss, the far doorway slid open and a denaidan female in a Syndicorp medical uniform stepped inside. Her gleaming copper skin and flowing brown hair reminded him of his mother, and a pang of loss twisted his gut. Then a sinister nudge wormed its way into his thoughts, urging him to relax. Snarling, he struggled past the numbing power of the cuffs to raise his ionic shield, drawing enough of it around his mind to silence the invading thoughts.

He met the woman's eyes, breathing hard from the exertion. "You're the one they called Dr. Dollard."

She smiled, teeth bright against her copper lips. "And you're the rebel called…" she glanced at a data pad in one hand. "Chigs. Served with the troopers for three years before going AWOL with the rest of your wretched breed."

Chigs scowled, but tried to keep his temper. This poor female was most likely another of Dollard's hybrids, duped into serving her late "father's" purpose. He had to make her see reason. "You're denaidan, too," he said. "One of us. Syndicorp annihilated our race, but there are a few of us left. Join us in the fight for justice."

She sneered and stepped gracefully toward his cell. "The continuation of my project is far more important than a race that is already all but dead."

This female had obviously been warped by her years in captivity. He wished more than ever that Emmy was here. She'd be able to show the woman that she was fighting for the wrong side. If Chigs kept trying to convince her, he'd probably just make things worse.

"Where's the human who was with me?" he asked instead.

Dollard waved a hand dismissively. "No longer your concern. She's been returned to her original purpose."

Uminaq. What did that mean? He wanted to grab this woman by the throat and throttle answers out of her. Since that wasn't an option, he tried to think like Emmy. *Be gentle,* he told himself. *Use your words, not your strength.*

"Was Dr. Dollard your father?" he asked, his voice sounding strangely hollow in his attempt at reining in his anger.

The woman laughed, the sound ringing off the metal walls and making the energy shield shimmer. "Oh, my, no. You are looking at Dr. Dollard—the original—given new life in this denaidan vessel."

The room seemed to tilt on its axis, making Chigs weak in the knees. Mind control was one thing, but moving an entire consciousness from one body to another? "Impossible," he gritted between clenched teeth.

She tapped the data pad against one palm. "The mind is but a living computer coded with cognitive patterns— memories, personality, knowledge. And the Synaptic Alteration Chamber I developed has turned out to have more applications than even I dreamed of. My team began tests using my consciousness as a prototype just before my initial body's untimely departure." She grinned. "Lucky for me."

"Ellam Cua," Chigs muttered, thinking of the foreboding laughter in his dreams. Dollard was still alive, not merely a haunting product of his subconscious memory.

The new Dr. Dollard leaned closer, apparently gleeful to continue bragging about his—her?—work. "We tested our methods on prisoners first—behavioral modifications, simple commands implanted into their minds, a cocktail of nanites to ensure the changes would take hold at a cellular level. Each species has a unique response to the treatments. Cyber sensitivity. Mind control. Telekinesis. But imagine my delight when we discovered that denaidan females could hold an entire consciousness. A perfect imprint."

A chill crept down Chigs's spine, his hands clenching into fists. "What happened to the female who actually owns that body?"

"Oh, she's long gone. The physical requirements of your barbaric breeding process erased her mind during our tests. But I've discovered a way to repurpose the flesh." Dollard gave her new body an appraising look, stroking her free hand over a breast and down her upper thigh as if stroking an animal she was considering for purchase. "Such a lovely host."

Chigs wanted to vomit. "The other denaidan females I met... are they like you, too?"

She smiled coldly. "I'm one of a kind—the first to have been fully integrated."

"You're an abomination!" Chigs's muscles tightened, urging him to spring for the doctor's throat, but he knew better than to try to breach the energy shield.

"I'm a pioneer," Dr. Dollard countered. "Evolving beyond the limitations of my flesh. With this technology, I shall live forever. The only problem is that hybrids don't offer a clean transfer, and my supply of pure denaidan females has grown woefully thin." She narrowed her eyes and looked at him like a predator assessing its prey. "But you've given me an unexpected solution."

"I'll die before agreeing to help you," Chigs vowed.

"Now, now. Don't be such a pessimist, Chigs," Dr. Dollard murmured, almost affectionately. "I think you'll quite enjoy what comes next for you. As the first male denaidan to join the project, you've opened up the possibility of producing more purebreds. Together, we can restore your race to a glory unlike any you could ever imagine."

Chigs recoiled, backing away until he hit the cell's rear wall. She wanted him to produce children for her to exploit? "Never!"

Dr. Dollard released an exaggerated sigh. "I advise you to reconsider. It took me years of trial and error to discover that denaidan females require an ionic pulse from a male to conceive, and although I developed a modulated frequency that will induce ovulation, my process leaves the female brain dead and sterile after just one birth. I have less than a handful of fertile females left. But now, with you here—"

"Stop!" Chigs shouted, his voice echoing off the walls. The thought of being used as a tool in Dr. Dollard's sickening experiments twisted his stomach. "I won't be a part of your atrocities. Even at the expense of my race."

Dr. Dollard reached into a pocket and removed a hypo-injector, regarding it critically, lips curving into a cruel smile. "There are ways of lowering your inhibitions and bending you to our will."

Chigs crossed his arms, every muscle in his body taut as he thought of Emmy. "denaidans mate for life, and I'm already bonded. Even with your drugs, my body is incapable of emitting the mating frequency with another woman."

Dr. Dollard huffed. "Don't try your lies with me. There are no denaidan females left outside this lab, and your mating frequencies are deadly to other species."

"Wrong." Chigs smirked, glad to finally have the upper hand. "Your own nanite experiments gave us the ability to mate with humans."

Interest flickered across Dollard's features, and she looked down at her data pad. A haughty smile curved her lips as she tapped something on the screen. "Ah, yes. The nanites I injected into that denaidan who broke into my cyborg lab. Noatak, I believe his name was. How fascinating. I always regretted not being able to follow up with that test subject."

Chigs watched Dollard scroll through items on the data pad, suddenly aware he'd made a serious blunder. Dollard hadn't known about their ability to mate with other species.

"This could open up new possibilities for our breeding program." Dollard speared Chigs with an avaricious look that sent chills down his spine. "How many of you have produced viable offspring?"

Thinking of Rashana, with a baby due any day now, Chigs shook his head. The previous Dr. Dollard had known about her pregnancy—had accelerated it, in fact. But this Dr. Dollard might not have that piece of memory, or assumed Rashana had perished. "I said mates, not children."

"Too bad." Dollard rubbed her chin, staring thoughtfully into the distance. "Though I can think of several things that might help facilitate reproduction. I've also been developing a dampening frequency that allows mating without solidifying a bond. I just need test subjects." Her gaze sharpened on Chigs once more. "But you say you're mated. Perhaps to that human we captured—the one you were so intent on protecting?"

Chigs's hearts began pounding a double drumbeat of impending doom. He focused on strengthening his empathic shield. His mother had been able to detect a lie even through his shielding, but he hoped this new Dr. Dollard wasn't as adroit at using the denaidan female ability. "Do you think I'd be foolish enough to bring my mate on a dangerous mission?"

Dollard raised an eyebrow. "I thought I was finished questioning dear Dr. Voss. I guess I was wrong."

With that, she turned and exited the brig.

Chigs stood breathing raggedly as he stared at the glimmering energy shield. He had to find a way out of this cell immediately.

240

Chapter Twenty-Five

Emmy glanced from the playing cards in her hand to one of the three denaidan females sitting around the table, trying to decide her next move. The woman's expression remained strangely robotic, even as she played a winning card. Although these women were physically similar to their male counterparts, with copper skin, dark hair, and high cheekbones, they lacked the boisterous camaraderie Emmy associated with the denaidan people. They seemed almost... hollow. Perhaps the females were simply that way.

Or it's because of the project.

The thought vanished as quickly as it had come, subsumed by her delight at being back on the team. Dr. Dollard had promised to bring Emmy up to speed and assign her some duties as soon as some administrative tasks had been handled.

Emmy countered her opponent's card with a double flip and smirked. She wasn't usually a competitive person, but she felt an almost visceral desire to best these women.

The next woman played her next card with efficient grace just as the common room door opened with a quiet hiss. The room fell silent, and in perfect unison, the women rose from their seats and retreated into the doors surrounding the common area. Emmy looked up to see Dr. Dollard standing at the entrance.

Unsure of how she was supposed to act in her new role, Emmy stood, laying her cards face down on the table. Her insides squirmed as Dollard moved to stand in front of her. "You may sit, Dr. Voss."

"Thank you." Emmy lowered herself stiffly back into her seat. The doctor had a way about her that commanded respect. Obedience.

"I have a few more questions, if you don't mind." The doctor's words felt almost hypnotic.

"Of course," Emmy said.

Dollard clasped her hands behind her back as if preparing to give a lecture. "How long have you been living among the rebels?"

A stubbornness rose inside Emmy, and she was tempted to refuse to answer. Hadn't she answered enough questions already? She tried to avert her gaze, but couldn't. "Half a cycle, I think."

"And what is it you do for the rebellion, exactly?" The doctor asked.

Emmy pressed her lips together, throat aching with words she didn't want to say. *Why am I feeling so uncooperative?* Despite her rising turmoil, her answer emerged from between her numb lips. "I provide counseling and mental health support when I can." She thought back to her frustration over the lack of interactions with the denaidan warriors. "Though to be honest, the denaidans haven't been very receptive to my help. I end up counseling the humans who've joined us more often."

The gleam in the doctor's coppery eyes sharpened. "I understand there are several denaidan males who have taken human mates."

Unease twisted inside Emmy like a live wire, yet her words continued to spill out. "A recent discovery involving nanites has altered the brain chemistry of the males, diminishing the destructive force of the mating bond. Three denaidans have mated with humans already, and the others are actively seeking human companions."

Dr. Dollard nodded. "I also understand that the mating bond between denaidans is permanent. Do you know if the same is true between humans and denaidans?"

"I don't believe that's been tested," Emmy said, her voice shaky. "Why?"

The doctor pursed her lips. "Restoring the denaidan race has become a top priority for Syndicorp."

Emmy frowned. "Why now?"

"We are going to rectify past mistakes, Dr. Voss. You want that, too, don't you?"

For some reason, a part of Emmy screamed that this was all lies. Yet she also wanted to believe denaidans were finally going to get the help they needed. She found herself nodding. "Yes, I do."

Dollard continued with a pointed question, "What is the nature of your relationship with Chigs?"

As if a dam had released, Emmy's thoughts about Chigs came flooding back: the first moment he'd walked into her office and asked for her help, the way his hand felt at the small of her back as they'd danced together, the cave where they'd made love... *He's my mate.* The acknowledgement landed like a punch to Emmy's gut.

Panting, she blinked at the doctor, who regarded her shrewdly. Why was Dollard asking her this? And what did it have to do with restoring the denaidan race?

"He's my mission partner," Emmy answered evasively.

"Is there nothing more between you?" Dollard pressed.

The weight crushing Emmy's will was almost unbearable, but she shook her head, teeth clamped over any further words. This was one secret she refused to share.

"Unfortunate." Dollard sighed, and the pressure on Emmy's mind slowly eased. "It would've been so much easier if his mate was here to assist."

"Make what easier?"

"Breeding him. I'd hoped we could use a seductive bait-and-switch. Now I'll have to resort to psychotropics to inhibit his resistance." The doctor pulled a data pad from her pocket and studied it.

Breeding him? Emmy's heart was racing fast enough to choke her. *But Chigs is mine.* Could the doctor really overcome the mating bond with drugs? The more Emmy focused on Chigs, the clearer her mind became.

Dollard wasn't interested in helping the denaidans out of altruism. She wanted the offspring. But why?

"What do you plan to do with the denaidan children?" Emmy asked.

Dollard slowly turned to face her. "You needn't concern yourself with the welfare of the children. I assure you, their well-being is necessary—vital, even—to the project."

The pressure to Emmy's mind resumed, but this time, she felt it coming and resisted. "Well-being? Or exploitation?"

"Exploit is such an ugly word," Dollard said reproachfully. "As scientists, our mission is to advance knowledge, to enhance life. Sometimes that requires a little exploration. You want to help improves life across the galaxy, don't you?"

Emmy swallowed thickly and nodded, surprised by that welling desire. *Why am I arguing?*

Dollard placed an icy hand on Emmy's shoulder. "Think of what we will achieve, the lives we will save. We will provide a future for the denaidans they never imagined possible. Tell me you're committed to make this succeed."

Emmy's heart fluttered with hope. She believed in the work she did for Syndicorp. Believed she could make the galaxy a better place. Despite the inner voice telling her not to trust the doctor's insidious words, she whole-heartedly wanted the denaidans to get the help they deserved. "I'm sorry I questioned you. I'm committed."

Dr. Dollard took Emmy's chill hands in her own. "Good. Now, before we proceed, is there anything else you'd like to tell me?"

Warmth spread from Dollard's hands up Emmy's arms, filling her chest, her head, her soul. There was one other thing Emmy had withheld during questioning besides that Chigs was her mate, and now seemed like the right moment to be honest. "Chigs and I hacked the mainframe and sent security codes to the *Icarus*," she blurted. "There's a team en route to extract the test subjects as we speak."

Dollard's features hardened, and her grip on Emmy's hands tightened. "I underestimated you, Dr. Voss. That won't happen again."

A spike of fear shot through Emmy's chest, only to be quickly numbed by a renewed vice grip around her will.

Dropping her hands, Dollard looked toward a pair of denaidan women who'd emerged from one of the door-ways. "Go check the mainframe."

As the women trotted from the room, Dollard accessed her datapad. "Dammit, they've already cleared the orbital weapon system and are nearing the base. Those damned cyborgs have been a thorn in my side since the moment I let Doug into the program. But with your help, the *Icarus* shall belong to me once again." Dr. Dollard tapped a finger against her lips thoughtfully. Emmy felt like she'd been cornered by a predator. "Do you still wish to avoid bloodshed, Dr. Voss?"

Though her nerves bristled with the desire to deny everything the doctor offered, Emmy nodded. "Yes."

"Good. I have a task for you. When your rebel friends arrive, you will be there to greet them. Tell them you're taking them to the captive females and escort them to the brig."

Emmy swallowed hard, a sickly taste coating her tongue. "But..."

Dollard crossed her arms. "It's the only way to save their lives. Understood?"

"Understood," Emmy replied, her voice hollow.

Rising, Emmy followed a denaidan female down the halls and up the elevator to the main entrance bay. A small spacecraft sat poised for departure, and banks of evacuation pods stood open and waiting. The denaidan left her sitting on an empty cargo box, staring at the bay door. Before too long, it hissed open, exposing a velvet swath of nighttime sky. Six figures moved cautiously into the light, each carrying a pulse weapon and encased in Syndicorp armor. She immediately recognized Tovik's copper hair and her friend Marlis's blond curls.

"You made it!" she called, standing to greet them.

Marlis scanned the surroundings with the keenness of an eagle, gripping both pistols at the ready. "No guards?"

"Where's Chigs?" asked Kashatok, a long pulse rifle in his hands.

Emmy's pulse quickened. *Captured!* But her lips refused to utter the word.

Rust stomped past her to glare toward the interior door. "That asshole left you alone?"

"The base was minimally guarded," Emmy said, wanting to vomit. But her body refused to do even that.

Marlis looked her up and down, a confused furrow between her brows. "He could've at least given you a gun."

Emmy thought of the weapon Chigs had handed her before they'd entered the common room, trying to recall where she'd left it. All she could see was Dr. Dollard's kind face urging her to save her friends.

"So where is he?" asked Kashatok again.

"Chigs is prepping the women to leave." The words came too easily, as if they weren't even hers. Her mind was a confusion of white noise. *Take them to the brig.* "We need to hurry."

Brushing off further questions, she led the team from the bay and down the hallways. The base echoed with silence, but as they rounded a corner, she spotted several denaidan females waiting near the guard room door, still dressed in blue tunics.

Tovik gasped and rushed toward the nearest woman. "Hi! We're here to save you!"

"Slow down, kid!" called Qaiyaan, but Tovik was already taking the woman's hand and following her through the door.

"Come," said another woman, her lips curved into an empty smile as she waited at the door.

Oblivious to the danger, Emmy's friends hurried forward. Emmy followed more slowly, her feet heavy.

"What the fuck?" Rust shouted as a pair of women crowded him into a cell.

Marlis's pistols were yanked from her grip. She threw a punch at the nearest woman, but the denaidan easily deflected the blow and sent Marlis crashing backwards into the cell. With chilling precision, the other females struck, their movements so swift and practiced that the team from the Icarus barely had time to react before the energy fields hummed to life, blocking their escape.

Emmy's hands trembled, and a lump swelled painfully in her throat. The disbelief and betrayal on her friends' faces cut through her sharper than any blade. Then she caught sight of Chigs staring at her from behind the glimmer of an energy shield, his expression a roiling mix of shock and grief.

What have I done?

CHAPTER TWENTY-SIX

It took all of Chigs's will not to slam himself against the barrier separating him from Emmy. The cool, blue light of the energy shield between them cast an ethereal glow over her features, enhancing the deadened focus in her eyes. She was here, standing almost within his reach—and yet she wasn't.

"Emmy, you must listen to me," he called out, at the same time trying to touch her through their mate bond. But the threads slipped from his grasp like beams of light.

Tovik was repeating, "We're not here to hurt you!" as the females who'd ambushed the team filed out of the brig.

Chigs couldn't see his friends trapped in the neighboring cells, but Rust's thunderous voice rattled the walls. "What the fuck is going on, Emmy?"

Emmy remained standing rigid at the center of the room. He could sense the struggle going on inside her, but there was nothing he could do about it from here. *If I could only touch her.* Then he might be able to summon enough ionic power to help her block Dollard's mental influence.

Rust shouted more obscenities.

"Calm down, Rust!" Chigs shouted back. "She's being mind controlled. Let me talk to her."

The cursing and confusion from the other cells quieted to tense muttering and pacing footsteps. Emmy opened her mouth, then stood there gaping as if she wanted to say something and couldn't.

Holding his cuffed hands tightly against his chest, Chigs moved close enough to the energy shield to feel its hum against his skin. "Emmy," he said with all the encouragement he could muster. "Your mind is being manipulated. Fight it. Please."

"Don't be ridiculous, Chigs." Her words felt forced, his name on her lips strained.

Only two denaidan women remained in the room now. The nearest one placed a hand on Emmy's shoulder. "Come with us, Dr. Voss."

Chigs watched a flicker of resistance cross Emmy's face, her muscles tensing slightly as if preparing to shrug off the touch. Hope surged in his chest. If she could still resist, even subconsciously, then she wasn't completely lost—not yet. "Stay with me, Emmy," he said. "Tell me what's going on."

Emmy slowly looked at the woman next to her. "Go on ahead. I need to discuss terms of cooperation between the rebels and Syndicorp."

A lump filled Chigs's throat. Cooperation? What was Dollard playing at? Despite the questions filling him, he kept silent. If he pushed too hard, his words might do the opposite of his intention.

The denaidan tilted her head as if listening to a far-away voice, then removed her hand from Emmy's shoulder. "Very well."

Pivoting, the woman exited, leaving Emmy alone to face the cells.

Chigs grinned. The more distance between her and the women, the weaker the mind control should be. As the last denaidan disappeared from view, he opened his mouth to speak, but Rust beat him to it.

"Tell us what's going on." The sound of a fist hitting a metal wall punctuated Rust's demand.

Emmy turned, looking away from Chigs into one of the other cells. "Syndicorp seeks a peaceful resolution with the rebellion." Her voice was steady, but her fingers twitched at her sides. "They want to make amends for past transgressions—to offer a future where we can coexist."

"Coexist?" Noatak laughed bitterly. "After everything they've done?"

"What the fuck, Emmy?" Marlis added. "You hate Syndicorp."

"I misunderstood their purpose."

"Emmy, this isn't you talking," Chigs said.

"Peace requires compromise," she countered, her tone taking on a forced edge. "I want to avoid any more bloodshed. Especially yours."

Chigs's hearts raced. The control over Emmy's mind was strong, twisting her genuine desires into a new direction she would have never agreed to. "You know better than anyone the lengths Syndicorp will go to maintain power. You've seen their atrocities firsthand."

Emmy's brow furrowed. Within her eyes swam a tumult of doubt, like a star struggling to shine through a nebula's dense haze.

"You can do it, Emmy!" he urged, allowing all the love he felt for her to seep into his words. "Remember who you are, what you stand for."

"Help us rescue these women," Tovik said.

Emmy's voice quivered with forced laughter, her agitation palpable even through the energy barriers. "Did they look like they need rescuing? They're stronger than they've ever been, not land-locked to some planet where they'll never achieve their full potential. For the first time in history, denaidan women are free."

Gut churning, Chigs said, "Those women are not free. Their minds are being controlled, just like yours is."

"Controlled? How?" Tovik asked, a question that was echoed in the other cells.

"One of Dollard's projects," Chigs said. He quickly recounted what he knew, including that Dollard had reanimated himself into the body of one of the women.

Mutters of shock and revulsion echoed through the neighboring cells. Throughout his explanation, Emmy's stoic expression never wavered, though her fingers now jittered at a faster pace.

"That bastard is alive?" Rust's voice ricocheted from every corner. "I knew it!"

The floor shook as Rust attacked the walls of his cell with renewed ferocity. Metal groaned, and the energy shield crackled, casting erratic shadows across Emmy's face. Her eyes widened, and she took a step backward toward the exit.

"Rust! Control yourself!" Chigs shouted over the commotion, but it was like whispering into a storm.

"Break, damn you!" Rust bellowed, continuing his assault on his prison.

Emmy pressed her hand to the control panel, and a blinding flash filled the air, sending a tingling shock-wave through the floor. Chigs wondered if Rust's brute force might've actually triumphed over technology. But then the solid thud of a body hitting the deck was followed by a silence as deafening as the outburst had been.

"Rust?" Tovik called out, his voice suffused with concern. "You okay, buddy?"

No response.

"Please don't make me do that to anyone else." Emmy stood motionless, one hand still poised over the brig's control panel.

A beat of shocked silence settled over the brig, then Marlis whispered, "Fuck. Emmy, did you kill him?"

"No." She licked her lips in a nervous gesture. "But the next shock might. Don't try to escape again."

Chigs gritted his teeth. The violence of Rust's attempted escape seemed to have fortified Emmy's belief in Syndicorp's cause. He closed his eyes briefly and murmured under his breath, "Ellam Cua, help me get through to her."

Keeping his voice calm but insistent, he said, "Remember who Dr. Dollard is. What he's done. The experiments, the manipulation. Rust was tortured by the doctor's very own hand." He wanted to reach through the energy shield and shake the truth into her, but forced himself to remain calm. "I'm sure the denaidan women here didn't volunteer to become test subjects, either."

Emmy's jaw set, her eyes hardening. "Yes, they did. We have the contracts to prove it. But that isn't the issue at the moment. Dr. Dollard wants to rectify Syndicorp's mistakes. He—she—wants to give the denaidan people a glorious future."

"Dollard wants to use me for some twisted breeding program," Chigs said, his voice shaking. "Are you really okay with that?"

Her eyes clouded with confusion and torment. "The continuation of your race is at stake, Chigs. This is bigger than you or me."

"I refuse to take part in Dollard's sick experiments. You're the only woman for me, Emmy. You're my mate."

Emmy's hands fluttered to her throat. "Remember your dream, Chigs. You're meant to be with one of these denaidans. It's your destiny—"

"No. Ellam Cua only revealed them to me so I'd find my way to you." He pleaded with every fiber of his being. "My destiny is with you, Emmy. And no one else."

Emmy wavered on her feet. "I'm saving your lives," she said. "You'll see."

She turned and stumbled toward the exit.

A wave of dread crashed over Chigs. He had to reach her. To touch her, even if it was the last time. "No! I refuse to accept this. Ellam Cua, give me strength."

Gritting his teeth in determination, he summoned what he could of his ionic power and slammed both fists against the energy shield. The room exploded with crackling light, engulfing his vision in a searing kaleidoscope of colors. Waves of electricity surged like a tidal wave through his veins, leaving him gasping for breath as it clenched his muscles and contorted his limbs. Focusing on their mate bond, he plowed forward through the storm, every muscle straining against the force of the barrier.

Emmy turned back and screamed, "Chigs! Stop, you'll kill yourself!"

He continued, knowing this was the only way he was going to reach her. Blue sparks of light clung to his skin like adhesive as he cleared the doorway, refusing to let go. The intensity of the agony searing through his body increased with every shuffling step forward. Even the restraint cuffs circling his wrists felt like they were going to burn through his bones. His vision swam with white-hot dots of pain, but all he could see was Emmy. "*Unqu akhala…*"

He managed one more step before collapsing to the ground, consumed by darkness.

Chapter Twenty-Seven

"No! Chigs!" Emmy cried out again, terror consuming her. She reached out and slapped her hand against the control panel, disabling the energy shield pulsing around his fallen body. The air stank of electricity and sweat.

Chigs lay sprawled and lifeless on the gray metal deck. The restraint cuffs he'd been wearing had released themselves, shorted out by the massive flow of energy.

Dropping to her knees, Emmy cupped his cheeks, staring in horror at the bruised hollows surrounding his eyes. She couldn't tell if he was breathing or not. "Don't be dead. Please!"

He is of no consequence. The unwelcome voice boomed through her thoughts, trying to regain control. *We have the others.* Her vision spun, and it felt as if the room had lost gravity. Grabbing hold of him like an anchor, she yelled, "Chigs is mine!"

Warmth surrounded her, stilling the confusion of thoughts. She looked down to see her mate's copper eyes open and focused on hers. Her soul thrummed with the vibrant connection of their bond. She sucked in a breath and threw her arms around him, pressing her forehead against his chest. "You're alive!"

His arms circled her shoulders, pulling her closer. "Emmy." His voice was rough as he cradled the back of her head, his hand threading through her hair. "You did it. You broke his control."

"I don't know what happened," she choked, regret seeping into every word. "I'm so sorry. I should have—"

"No apologies," Chigs said sternly and kissed the top of her head.

An insistent voice cut through their reunion. "Emmy!" Tovik yelled. "Open our cells."

She looked up at her friends, lit by the sickly green glow of the energy shields. The entire mission had been undermined because of her weakness. She'd delivered her friends straight to their enemy's hands. Then she remembered what she'd done to Rust. "Rust! Are you okay?"

She started to stand, but Chigs grabbed her arm. "You need to stay in physical contact with me. Dollard's mind control will find you once you're out of my ionic shield, and I'm not strong enough to extend it very far."

Her throat tightened, fear once again swelling within her. This really was all her fault. "Right."

She helped Chigs struggle to his feet. He had to lean on her, his muscles still twitching, but they hobbled to the nearby control panel and dropped the cell barriers. Everyone except Rust came rushing out. While Noatak and Qaiyaan checked on Rust, Tovik offered Emmy a pendant on a silver chain. "Here, put this on."

"What is it?" An oblong silver bauble the size of her thumb glowed with tiny green and blue lights that sparkled like gems.

"The device Rashana and I were working on to block her mind control. Sorry I didn't have it ready before you and Chigs left the *Icarus*."

She took the pendant, expecting to feel a low buzz or other sensation that something was happening, but there was nothing. "Are you sure it works?"

"I think so. Marlis and Rust are wearing them and are still themselves."

Just then, Rust stumbled from his cell, head clutched in both cybernetic hands. "Fuck! Emmy—"

Chigs angled his body protectively between her and the cyborg. "Don't blame her."

"I ain't gonna hurt her," Rust grumbled, but stopped in his tracks. "You okay Emmy?"

"I… yes." She peered around Chigs to examine Rust's hard face. "Are you?"

He shrugged. "Dollard's done worse to me." Then he scowled at Chigs. "You were supposed to keep Emmy inside your shielding to protect her. What happened?"

"It was a mistake. The test subjects all looked like normal denaidans." Chigs said. "My guard was down." He stood with his back against the wall, his face still creased with residual pain.

Emmy squeezed his hand, leaning her shoulder against his to lend her support. "I think Dollard is controlling their minds, too."

She quickly explained what she knew about the test subjects, including Dollard's assertion that the women had joined the project voluntarily.

"*Uminaq!*" Kashatok swore. "Those bastards really were taking women off Denaida-daru!"

"You knew about this?" asked Noatak.

Kashatok's features were dark with fury. "In my younger days, I... knew a female who fell for Syndicorp's lies. She wanted to travel the stars." His voice sounded strained, and Emmy sensed there was likely more to the story. "But Ayana died before Syndicorp got her off the planet."

Qaiyaan put a hand on Kashatok's shoulder. "Now is not the time for self-recrimination, *iluq*. Now is the time for revenge."

"How?" asked Chigs. "Doug must've lost control over the security systems, or he'd have freed us."

"At least he got us inside," said Qaiyaan. "We can handle it from here."

"I personally volunteer to pound every Syndicorp puppet on this base to a pulp." Rust flexed his cybernetic arms. At least he looked none the worse for wear after being knocked out.

Tovik held up his hands. "Hold on. The test subjects are under mind control like Emmy. We need to find a way to free them, not hurt them."

"We were told that there are sixteen test subjects," said Chigs. "There aren't enough of us here to provide ionic shielding for that many."

"You won't need to." Tovik's eyes were alight with excitement. "If we can reach the mainframe, I can try to splice one of the pendants in and boost the broadcast. That should free anyone in the compound still under Dollard's control. I might even be able to get Doug back into the system."

"That's a pretty big set of ifs," said Qaiyaan.

"And what if we run into more females before we reach the mainframe?" asked Rust. "The ones we met were surprisingly efficient at disarming us."

"We've all been trained in using non-lethal force," said Marlis, casting a meaningful glance toward Rust.

Everyone else nodded. Rust grunted noncommittally before shrugging. "Sure."

"Good. Let's get moving," said Qaiyaan. "Dollard's probably already regrouping after losing control of Emmy. Take out any surveillance equipment you see."

At Qaiyaan's signal, Emmy touched the control panel and opened the door to the brig, bracing herself for an onslaught of armed guards. But the hall outside was completely empty. With a sigh of relief, she took Chigs's hand and motioned for everyone to follow her as she tiptoed down the corridor, her footsteps barely making a sound. As they approached the elevator, the doors opened. Out stepped half a dozen guards in full battle gear, followed by one test subject in her simple blue tunic and pants. They all held pulse rifles.

Rust charged forward.

Tovik bolted after him, shouting, "Non-lethal!"

The guard Rust was targeting sidestepped, using Rust's momentum to send him sprawling onto the floor. A bright blue light lit the air as another guard fired at the cyborg. Rust rolled out of the way, barely escaping the blast. A charred patch marred the deck where he'd been less than a heartbeat earlier.

Tovik tackled another guard, driving him against the wall, while Kashatok swept the legs out from under a third. The guard's pulse rifle clattered to the floor, skidding back into the open elevator.

Marlis and Noatak moved in as Kashatok used his ionic shielding to deflect pulse fire, while Qaiyaan followed just behind, sending shockwaves of ionic energy at the enemies with a force that made the hallway sound like the nexus of a thunderstorm. The air reeked of ozone and hot metal.

A bolt from one rifle zinged off Chigs's shielding and punched a hole through a wall panel overhead, making Emmy cringe.

"We need to find cover!" Chigs shouted, pulling her toward a nearby door in the hall.

Emmy pressed her palm to the control, relieved when the door slid open to reveal an empty office. Chigs pushed her inside and pointed to the solitary desk in the middle of the room. "Hide behind that."

"Wait!" she shouted as he rushed back to the hallway.

She edged toward the door and chanced a look around the corner. Nearby, Chigs grappled with one guard, knocking the rifle from the man's grip. Marlis and Noatak were near the elevator, fighting back-to-back in a flurry of kicks and punches. Kashatok blocked blows from a combat knife, blue blood coating his arm. Pulse fire strafed past the doorway, forcing Emmy to duck back inside.

Frustrated by her lack of usefulness, she frantically searched the office for a weapon, but came up empty-handed. The desk and shelves were bare, not even an abandoned paperweight. Sounds of pulse blasts and grunts of pain continued outside.

Returning to the door, she peeked outside again. Tovik struggled with the denaidan woman, trying to twist her rifle from her grip. She brought her knee to his groin, doubling him over, then crashed the butt of the gun against his head. Tovik stumbled and fell to his knees.

Two guards were now forcing Chigs backward. A bolt of light whizzed dangerously close to his ear, and he bared his teeth, crossing his forearms in front of him as if it was taking all his strength to keep his shield in place.

Her gaze snagged on an abandoned pulse rifle on the floor near the other side of the hallway. If she was lucky, she might reach it and get back to the office in one piece. She glanced toward the fight again just as a pulse bolt hit Qaiyaan square in the chest, sending him flying past her doorway. He skidded down the hall in a crumpled heap.

The guard who'd shot him looked up and spotted her standing there. He swung his barrel in her direction. Emmy's heart thudded a rapid pace inside her. If she retreated, she'd be trapped and helpless.

Drawing on all her courage, she dove for the rifle across the hall, sliding on her belly, hands outstretched to clasp the barrel. Her fingers found the trigger, and she swiveled, aiming back toward the door of the office. With no time to second-guess herself, she fired.

A pulse of light zinged from the rifle's barrel, missing the guard but causing him to duck.

Emmy rolled onto her side and took aim again. Her heart pounded in her chest as she lined up the crosshairs on the attacker. She squeezed the trigger again, this time hitting her mark squarely in the chest. The guard dropped his weapon and staggered back against the wall before crumpling to the floor.

Emmy pushed herself to a kneeling position, heartbeat drowning out the sounds of battle. *I killed someone.* Blinking back hot tears, she gripped the rifle tighter and quickly took aim at the guards closing in on Chigs. Her body shook with adrenaline and terror as she waited for a clear shot. She fired, hitting one guard in the back and sending him sprawling.

Chigs took the opening to deliver a killing blow to the last guard before glancing in Emmy's direction. His eyes widened in surprise and something akin to approval as he spotted her.

Then, to her horror, she saw the denaidan female charge him from behind, a blood-coated blade in her hands. In less than a second, that blade would drive straight into Chigs's back. *Fuck this non-lethal bullshit.*

Gritting her teeth, she raised the rifle and took aim.

Chapter Twenty-Eight

Chigs's eyes widened as Emmy aimed her rifle directly at him, his hearts threatening to explode. Was she mind controlled again? Then he realized she wasn't aiming at him—he was aiming behind him. He spun in time to block a blow from the denaidan female's knife. With a focused ionic blast, he sent her staggering backward.

She tripped over a fallen guard and landed hard on her back next to Tovik.

Staggering slightly and bleeding from his temple, Tovik took advantage of her momentary daze and lunged forward, pinning her to the ground. Meanwhile, Rust ended his struggle by lifting a guard overhead and slamming him down onto the ground with a sickening crunch. Kashatok, covered in sweat and blood, elicited a blood-curdling scream as he drove his blade into the side of one guard, then turned to another. And like the sudden turning of a tide, Marlis and Noatak also took down their adversaries in perfect synchronization.

Just like that, the battle was over.

Chigs's gaze frantically sought Emmy in the residual chaos, double hearts hammering. *Please tell me she's survived this.* He spotted her crouched behind Qaiyaan, helping him sit up.

Hurrying toward the pair, he snagged Emmy's arm and pulled her to her feet. "What in the name of Ellam Cua were you thinking?" His words were harsher than intended, his hearts still pounding with adrenaline and relief. "You could have been killed!"

Emmy blinked at him, wide-eyed, her face pale and her body trembling slightly. The rifle was slung over her shoulder against her back. "We were losing, Chigs. I had to help." She yanked her arm out of his grip. "Go check on Tovik."

A wave of admiration washed over him. His mate might not be a warrior, but she was a force to be reckoned with. He turned to find Tovik arguing with the denaidan female.

"Please, stop!" said the woman. "I'm on your side!"

"Then why the hell did you attack us?" Tovik released her and stood.

"*Uminaq!* Do not release her, Tovik!" Chigs shouted. "She's mind controlled!"

"No, she's not. I put my shielding around her," Tovik said.

Chigs watched the woman as she backed away, her previous soldier persona replaced by over-exaggerated sobbing. "I'm not sure it worked, kid."

"We thought you were more of Dollard's men," she said between wails. "We panicked when you rushed us."

Rust moved in behind her and grabbed her arms. "That wasn't panic." He began tying her wrists behind her. "That was a coordinated attack."

The woman moaned in pain, and Tovik glowered, fists balling at his sides. "Take it easy, asshole. She's injured."

"Don't tell me what to do." Rust didn't look up from his task, but his touch seemed to gentle sightly.

"Please don't let him hurt me." The woman kept her eyes locked with Tovik's, like she knew he was the weakest link.

Unease churned in Chigs's stomach. "We're not going to hurt you, but we need to keep you restrained," he said as he tore a strip from the edge of her tunic and shoved it against her teeth, tying it tight behind her head. "You can forgive me later."

"Do you really need to gag her?" asked Tovik. "That seems extreme."

"We can't have her screaming for help." Chigs looked at the woman. "You understand, right?"

She thrashed her head, her muffled words full of obvious vitriol.

Tovik patted her gently on the shoulder. "You'll be back to yourself soon, and then we can free you. I promise."

She glared back at him. Chigs was fairly certain if she could've bitten the kid, she would've.

Chigs and Emmy guided the group onto the elevator and, from there, down the hallway toward the stairs. He didn't like how quiet the base was. The group who attacked them couldn't have been all of Dollard's guards. And where were the denaidan women? They'd seemed to be an integral part of Dollard's team. Though he had to admit he was glad there weren't more denaidan women involved in the battle. He only prayed they found them soon and that Tovik's device worked as planned.

The captured denaidan woman trudged down the stairwell, face sullen. Tovik kept giving her lovesick glances. The poor kid never seemed to catch a break. Chigs reflected on how strange it was that at one point he'd expected to find a mate among these females. Now his duty to rescue them for the sake of his people was overshadowed by his fierce desire for Emmy; he'd do whatever it took to protect her.

His dual hearts pounded as they emerged from the stairwell into the long hall leading to the mainframe in the bowels of the facility. The metallic walls felt like they were pressing in on all sides, held back by a coiled spring ready to snap. Ahead, past a few closed doors, the door to the mainframe stood ajar, a crack of light spilling into the hallway.

"That's it." Chigs pointed. "Through that doorway."

"Dollard probably posted guards in there," added Emmy, radiating regret. "I let it slip about Doug cracking the security firewalls while he had me under mind control."

"It wasn't your fault," said Chigs, taking her hand and squeezing.

She nodded, but he knew she still felt weighted with guilt.

Kashatok and Tovik scouted ahead, pausing near the door to listen. After a tense moment, Kashatok pushed it fully open with one hand, revealing the bright lights of humming servers inside. Chigs's eyes immediately darted to the spot where the dead guard had lain, but there was no sign of the body and no additional guards.

"That's strange." Emmy pressed herself against his side. "Why isn't it guarded?"

"Maybe those guys on the elevator were it," suggested Tovik hopefully. He looked at the bound woman for verification, but she just stared at him sullenly.

Rust clomped around the glowing server. "Dollard's a spineless rat. He probably triggered the auto-destruct and is scurrying to the shuttle bay like a coward."

"*Uminaq*. I didn't consider that. I'd better check." Tovik plopped down at a console. After a couple of breathless minutes, he stood again. "No self-destruct that I can see."

"Fuck, kid, you barely looked," said Rust. "Do I have to do everything?" He yanked a panel from one side of the console and planted a hand against the bare wiring. His cybernetic eye flashed green, then gold, as he used his cyber sensitivity to scan the system.

Chigs scratched his beard, keeping one eye on the denaidan woman. Her eyes remained locked on Tovik, but her face showed no emotion. If there was a self-destruct counting down, was she capable of caring?

"I need one of you to give up your pendant so I can tie it into the mainframe," said Tovik.

Emmy pulled hers free. "Use mine. Both Marlis and Rust would be far more dangerous under mind control."

Marlis punched her shoulder lightly. "I wouldn't say that. Look how you handled yourself in that last fight."

Chigs would've preferred Emmy that keep the device, but giving up hers was the most logical option. "Just remember to stick close to me, no matter what," he reminded her. Then he leveled a pointed stare toward Tovik. "This plan better work."

Tovik rolled his eyes. "Stop being such a doubter." He cast a smile toward the denaidan female. "Once I'm done with this, I'll be able to untie you."

She nodded, though her eyes remained cold. Tovik beamed back. Chigs prayed this worked, or the kid was going to be heartbroken.

Pendant in hand, Tovik opened a nearby control panel and leaned inside. After a few moments of fiddling, he emerged, features pinched in thought, and he moved to the nearest console. His fingers danced over the keyboard, seconds bleeding into minutes that felt like hours.

Rust pulled his hand from the wiring. "Kid was right. No self-destruct."

"Told you," Tovik mocked in a sing-song voice as his fingers continued flying over the controls.

With a last flourish, he pressed a key and spun to look triumphantly at his team. At the same moment, the denaidan woman collapsed, crumpling to the ground like a marionette with its strings cut. Emmy gasped, her fingers digging into Chigs's forearm.

"What happened?" Qaiyaan demanded.

Kashatok dropped to a knee and pressed his fingers to the woman's throat. "She's alive."

Noatak glowered at Tovik. "What did you do?"

Tovik shook his head, his face ashen in the flashing lights from the computers. "I boosted the signal through the comm system. It should've freed her from Dollard's control." He turned an angry glare toward Rust. "You must have messed with the system while you were in there!"

Rust raised both hands. "I didn't change any programming. Only looked."

Letting out a shaky breath, Tovik focused back on the mainframe console, poking again at the controls. "Come on, come on," he muttered under his breath, desperation coloring his words. He stopped typing and spun to look at the denaidan woman again. "Okay. I turned off the signal pulse. Is she back?"

Kashatok pulled back the woman's eyelids one at a time. "Still non-responsive."

With a frustrated growl, Tovik slammed his fist against the console. "I don't know what else to do!"

"Did this happen to everyone on the base?" asked Noatak in a quiet monotone Chigs had learned to recognize as deadly serious.

Tovik nodded, his voice trembling. "Everyone within a hundred meters of a comm unit that had been mind controlled like she was."

Chigs felt like he had been punched in the gut as he started to put everything together. "What if these females didn't have minds to control?" Dollard had said the woman whose body he inhabited had been "long gone." Brain dead after the abominable attempts to use her for breeding. Had that been the fate of all the test subjects? "What if they were… possessed, like the female Dollard?"

Silence filled the room, made heavier by the hum of the mainframe.

Emmy's fingers gently brushed a strand of hair from the woman's face. "Then we freed them from slavery. I know I'd rather die than live controlled like I was."

"Are you saying that the body Dollard was using is probably just like these now?" asked Kashatok.

"Fuuuuck!" shouted Rust. "I need to find that bastard and finish him myself!" Before anyone could react, he stormed out of the room, his heavy footsteps echoing down the corridor.

Emmy rose, her lips in a grim line. "Dollard mentioned something about women still in cryo pods. I was supposed to help prepare them for..." She swallowed distastefully. "Breeding. But I think it means their minds are still intact."

Qaiyaan ran a hand over his face, his expression grim. "Assuming Dollard hasn't done his usual cut and run, taking them with him. We should split up and secure the rest of the base."

"There may still be Syndicorp guards," Kashatok said. "Keep your shields up."

Tovik's gaze swung between the collapsed female and the door. "What about this female? What if she wakes up?"

"I don't think she will, Tovik," said Kashatok. "Mek hasn't been able to wake the ones back on the *Icarus*."

"But we can't just leave her here," Tovik insisted, his ginger brows furrowed in worry. "What if there are more Syndicorp guards? Or if Dollard isn't dead and comes back?"

"We'll carry her with us," Chigs said. "We'll get all the females out of here, brain dead or otherwise. It's the least we can do."

"I'll carry her," said Tovik with a crack in his voice. He lifted the female into his arms as if she were spun glass.

As they headed for the door, Chigs prayed to Ellam Cua that they could find the females—and that they were still alive.

CHAPTER TWENTY-NINE

Emmy swallowed hard and clutched her rifle to her chest, sticking close to Chigs as they left the low hum of the mainframe room. Shadows blanketed the cold metallic corridor, and they moved cautiously, Kashatok taking point and opening doors with a quick ionic pulse to each control pad. All they found were empty offices and dusty storage rooms.

With hurried steps, they ascended the stairs, footsteps echoing against the walls. At the top, Rust's scowling face greeted them, cybernetic gaze cutting through the dim light. "This level's clear. Not a damned guard anywhere." A muscle along his jaw twitched as if he was grinding his teeth. "If Dollard's still here, we can't let him escape. Let's head to the shuttle bay."

Emmy glanced toward the comatose female in Tovik's arms. Could Dollard possibly still be alive?

"We can't expose our backs," said Qaiyaan as they stepped inside the elevator. "Marlis, Noatak, and Kashatok with me. We'll get off on the next level. You four keep going."

"Emmy's not combat trained," Chigs argued, putting a protective arm around her shoulders. "And Tovik's got his hands full. That's half our team."

A spark of defiance flared in Emmy's chest. "I can handle myself." She tightened her sweaty grip around her rifle. "You saw me drop that guard earlier. I'll stick close so you can shield me. We'll be fine."

Chigs reluctantly agreed. "If Dollard is still alive, you can bet he won't be easy to find. Watch for traps."

The door slid open, allowing the first group to exit. Emmy focused on her breathing as they rode to the next floor.

When the elevator doors opened again, Rust stepped out first, looking up and down the corridor. "You three go that way and watch our back. I'll go down here toward the shuttle bay."

Emmy realized they were on the level where she and Chigs had first encountered the test subjects. She put a hand on the cyborg's forearm. "Remember, there could still be innocent people on the base. Not just denaidan women. Keep in mind what we've talked about in therapy. Think before you react."

He scowled, but nodded sharply. "Understood." Without another word, Rust turned and started down the adjoining corridor, cybernetic footsteps loud in the empty space.

Emmy trailed Chigs down the corridor in the opposite direction, trying not to step on his heels, while Tovik brought up the rear. She had to admit, she was feeling rather anxious about revisiting the room where Dollard had violated her mind. Then again, there was a good chance the doctor might be there. She wasn't sure which outcome she hoped for—meeting Dollard and the other test subjects alive and prepared for battle, or discovering them as comatose husks of the women they should have been.

As they approached the long window, Chigs's steps slowed, then stopped. Through their mate bond, she felt his heightened emotions flutter with grief. Emmy's stomach clenched. She peered around him through the glass, seeing bodies littering the floor inside. "Oh, no."

Tovik came around her to look, and his face turned pale beneath his ginger beard. "Is that... all of them?" he asked.

Chigs sighed heavily. "We need to go inside and take a tally."

He opened the door, and Emmy placed a hand on the woman in Tovik's arms. "You don't have to go in there," she said softly. "Chigs and I can handle it."

Tovik swallowed hard. "If there's anyone left behind, I want to be there."

A pang of empathy lanced through Emmy's chest. His unwavering optimism touched her deeply. Chigs had once dreamed of finding his mate here, and Tovik had been no less hopeful. *He's had so many let downs.* She'd counseled Tovik several times, helping him set realistic expectations, and she had to admire his resilience.

She placed a hand on his shoulder. "I'm here if you need me."

They followed Chigs inside, weapons ready in case there were guards waiting in ambush.

Denaidan females lay strewn across the floor like discarded dolls, their copper faces slack and empty. Their bodies still lived, but their minds were dead. Emmy shuddered, wondering if this might've been her destiny if she hadn't broken Dollard's control over her.

Tovik gently set the woman he was carrying on a nearby exam table and began checking the others for life signs.

His face looked haggard as he sank to one knee beside a young woman with thick, brown hair. "Rest well, dear one," he said softly.

Emmy fought to compartmentalize her own rush of anguish. She could feel his heart breaking anew as he repeated the phrase over and over, arranging awkward limbs and straightening clothing.

She followed behind Chigs as he finished checking the nearby rooms for guards. Every room was empty. "No Dollard," said Chigs, watching Tovik move to the next fallen female. "We need to keep moving."

"Give him a moment," she said as Tovik as lifted the female from a chair and laid her gently on the floor.

Tovik glanced at them. "You two go on. I want to stay and protect them until we're sure the base is clear."

"All right," said Chigs, his tone softening. "Keep an eye out for guards."

Leaving Tovik behind might not have been the most strategic choice, but it felt like the right one. These women would likely never regain consciousness, but they were still precious to the denaidans, symbolic of the past that had been taken from them forever.

She and Chigs opened doors along the corridor, finding empty offices, storage rooms, and abandoned labs.

There had been ongoing experiments here only a short time ago, but their intel had indicated the lab was in the process of moving. Could the remaining staff have fled so quickly? Or—even worse—could Dollard have escaped with them?

Ahead, the corridor ended at a massive bay door with a long, narrow window. Emmy moved forward, standing on her tiptoes next to Chigs to peer through the glass. On the other side lay a bullet-shaped, translucent pod, its interior glowing with golden light.

She exhaled raggedly. "That's one of Dollard's SAC units. The ones he used to wipe a test subject's mind." Her stomach clenched as she also realized it was likely the device that allowed Dollard to insert his consciousness into another body.

Chigs cupped his hands around his face and continued looking through the glass. "I don't see anyone inside. You'd think this technology would be well guarded." He stepped back. "Stay behind me while I open the door."

Emmy stepped behind Chigs, pulse hammering in her ears as he shorted out the door control. The hydraulics lifted with a metallic groan, and a musty, clinical stench wafted out, as if the very air had been poisoned by malevolence.

Rifle aimed and ready, Chigs waited for several heartbeats. Only silence responded. Finally, he said, "Let's take a look."

The cavernous bay swallowed the sound of their footsteps as they approached the SAC unit. It stood on a high platform at one end of a long row of cryopods, looking like a matriarch's cocoon, its smooth curves glowing with light from within. Terrified she might find some hapless soul trapped inside, Emmy climbed the steps onto the platform. The unit was empty, its sterile interior like a dark maw waiting for its next victim.

She exhaled in relief. "Empty."

Using her higher vantage point, she looked down the row of cryopods. They all glowed with faint light, but she couldn't see through the small windows from here. Thick wires snaked from each pod, rising upward until they entered a wide conduit embedded high on the wall. The ceiling panels were arranged in a way that resembled a giant iris, giving the impression that it could open and close just like a door.

She hopped down and followed Chigs along the row, checking inside each. Unlike the SAC unit, the cryopods were occupied; one enayshuan, a posungi... and three denaidans.

"They're alive," Chigs said, reverence hushing his tone.

Emmy grinned, feeling shaky with joy. "Tovik's going to be thrilled."

Then Chigs swore, looking closely at the pod's control panel. "*Uminaq.* Is that an auto destruct timer?"

Emmy pushed past him to look closer. A digital timer on the display was ticking down from twenty minutes. She tapped in a query, then glanced toward the ceiling, realizing why it looked like an iris. Most cryopods could double as escape pods. "It looks like Dollard programmed them to eject!"

"Can you stop it?" Chigs asked.

Emmy tapped at the controls, but was denied access to command controls. "I'm locked out."

"We didn't come this far just to lose them again," he growled. He activated his comm. "We've got denaidan survivors on level three, but it looks like—"

His sentence cut off as light flashed overhead and the air vibrated with the repercussion of a pulse blast.

Chapter Thirty

Emmy's breath rushed from her lungs as Chigs grabbed her around the waist and dove behind the nearest empty pod. More searing blasts scarred the floors and walls on either side.

She caught sight of their attacker just before the pod blocked her view. "Rust, stop! It's us! Chigs and Emmy!"

Another blast seared past the pod.

"Rust? What the hell?" Chigs shouted.

"Denaidan filth." Rust's voice sounded odd, less angry and more automated. "You're only delaying the inevitable."

Suddenly Emmy knew where she'd heard that voice before—inside her own mind. Her blood turned to ice water. "He's being controlled!"

Horror widened Chigs's eyes. "Dollard."

Confusion and disbelief coiled in Emmy's gut. "But how? The pendant should protect him."

Chigs shook his head. "I don't know."

Rust's heavy footfalls shook the floor as he advanced, filling the air with blue bolts of light.

"We've got to pierce his armor. Set your rifle to kill," Chigs yelled over the cacophony, risking a glance around his cover. A blast scorched the edge of the pod, making him flinch back.

"No!" Emmy shouted. "He's being mind controlled. We need to find Dollard and break the connection."

Chigs looked at her like she was insane. "Rust's as armored as a battle cruiser. The only way we're getting past him is by killing him."

"He's family, Chigs," she pleaded, glad to see the reluctant acknowledgement in Chigs's eyes. "Do you think you can use your ionic shield to disrupt the mind control?"

Chigs grabbed her hand and dragged her around the pod to keep it between them and Rust. "I'd have to get close enough to touch him, which would mean leaving you unprotected, not only from pulse fire, but from Dollard's mind control."

"Like I pointed out earlier, Rust's far more dangerous to us than I am under Dollard's control." Emmy flinched as another blast shook the room. "We need to try."

A massive form loomed around the corner, cybernetic eyes settling on them. Chigs thrust Emmy behind him, his ionic shield glittering with power.

"Emmy, run!" he shouted, charging headlong at the hulking cyborg.

Rust stepped back, clearly caught off guard by the bold frontal assault. His rifle fired wildly, splashing the floor with energy blasts.

Emmy turned and dashed down the row of pods toward the bay door. Stray pulse blasts from Rust's weapon lit the air.

Looking for cover, Emmy climbed up onto the platform next to the SAC unit and lay down, hoping to remain out of sight from the ground as she peered over the edge.

The two warriors collided in a blur of metal and muscle, and Rust landed a brutal punch to Chigs's midsection, knocking the wind from his lungs. Chigs staggered back, gasping.

Emmy gasped, too. She'd watched the guys from the *Icarus* spar countless times and had been confident Chigs could hold his own long enough to use his shield on Rust. But this fight was far more intense than any she'd seen in the ring. *What if Chigs loses?* Her stomach heaved at the thought.

Hoping to distract the cyborg and give Chigs a chance to recover, she shouted. "Rust, stop! Don't let Dollard control you like this. You're stronger than he is!"

Rust ignored her, bringing his rifle to bear and squeezing the trigger.

Chigs raised his ionic shield, deflecting the blasts. There didn't seem to be an opening for him to let down his shield long enough to bring Rust inside, at least not without getting shot.

Feinting left, Chigs ducked in to drive his fist up toward Rust's chest. Emmy recalled the guard in the hallway, killed by just such a punch, and her stomach dropped.

Rust twisted away, and Chigs's blow slammed into the nearby cryopod, cratering the metal surface. Before Chigs could recover, Rust's cybernetic arm whipped around, catching Chigs square in the jaw.

The blow lifted Chigs off his feet, flinging him across the room to crash in a heap against the far wall. He struggled to his hands and knees, coughing. Blood ran from his forehead into his eyes.

Rust widened his stance and took aim.

With a heavy heart, Emmy set her rifle to the highest level and pointed it at the cyborg. If she had to kill Rust to save Chigs, she would, though she knew it would haunt her for the rest of her days.

Then the insidious slither of a command probed the edge of her mind. *Shoot the filthy denaidan.*

The barrel of her rifle slid toward Chigs as if it had a life of its own.

Oh, hell no.

With a painstaking effort of will, Emmy shoved the words out of her mind and let go of the rifle. Best not to have it in her hands. Pushing to her hands and knees, she scoured the area for any sign of Dollard.

The doctor stood on the other side of the platform, aiming a pulse pistol toward Emmy. *You need the rifle.*

"Get out of my head," Emmy snarled, rising to her feet.

The scientist's expression twisted in rage. Dollard squeezed off a blast from the pulse pistol, sending a searing bolt past Emmy's head. Ears ringing, Emmy flung herself to the side, hit the top step, and tumbled down the rest of the stairs. Her shoulder cracked against the bottom tread, making her arm go numb and sending her rifle clattering across the floor.

"Fuck." Emmy struggled to stand.

Dollard advanced, graceful in her stolen denaidan body, pulse pistol aimed at Emmy's face.

Knowing she'd never reach her gun in time, Emmy charged, her petite frame driving into Dollard's middle. She grabbed behind the doctor's knees and toppled her over backward, landing on top. The pistol clattered across the deck, and the doctor swore.

As Emmy grappled for control, Dollard cinched her legs around Emmy's waist and flipped them to take the top. With her weight pinning Emmy down, she grabbed Emmy's throat and squeezed. "You've outlived your usefulness after all, Dr. Voss."

Shoulder throbbing, Emmy tried to get her arms up between the doctor's wrists to break her grip, but their bodies were too close together. Spots danced across her vision. Then she remembered an old lesson Marlis had taught her. *Every inch of your body is a weapon. Use it.*

With the last of her rapidly fading strength, Emmy slammed her forehead up into Dollard's face. The impact jarred the scientist's grip, giving Emmy a split second to bring her hands up and break free. Gasping for air, she clawed at Dollard's eyes, forcing the doctor back.

Emmy seized her chance and swiftly rolled out of reach. Her hand found Dollard's gun, its weight giving her a sense of power. She spun and fired off a shot that hit Dollard square in the chest.

Dollard buckled. Wheezed. Then glared at Emmy defiantly. "My consciousness... transcends... this flesh..." Her voice was little more than a ragged whisper as her body went limp and the life faded from her eyes.

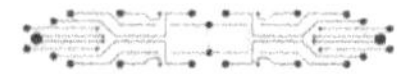

Chigs had just dodged another of Rust's skull-splitting blows when suddenly the cyborg stopped moving and stood still, a vacant expression crossing his features. Chigs saw his chance and opened his shield, reaching to pull him in.

Rust let out a furious bellow and charged past him, his eyes blazing with rage and determination.

Stunned and off balance, Chigs turned to see Emmy lying on the floor near the SAC unit. She held a pistol aimed at a crumpled body a short distance away.

Ignoring the ache in his leg where Rust had landed a particularly hard blow, he dashed forward after Rust. If that damned cyborg harmed a hair on Emmy's head…

But the cyborg ignored Emmy and grabbed the other figure, hoisting it up like a rag doll and shaking it furiously. It was Dr. Dollard—or the body that had once hosted Dollard. The body that now stared lifelessly at the floor.

"I should've been the one to do it!" Rust shouted, throwing the body back to the floor. He lifted one heavy foot, preparing to stomp down on the woman's head.

"That isn't Dollard, Rust. Not anymore," Emmy said from where she lay on the ground.

Rust hesitated a moment, then lowered his foot. Swearing loudly, he stomped off down the hall. "I need something to punch."

Fairly certain the cyborg was no longer a threat, Chigs scooped Emmy into his arms. "Are you okay? What happened?"

"She came out of nowhere." Emmy blinked, the shock fading from her eyes and a grin taking over. "But I fought her off."

Chigs laughed and hugged her tightly. "Yes, you did, *akhala.*"

Chapter Thirty-One

Chigs worked tirelessly with the team to bring the heavy cryopods onto the *Icarus*, carefully maneuvering them through the narrow corridors to the med bay.

"When can we talk to them?" asked Tovik hopefully, staring at one of the denaidan females. He wasn't the only male looking at the females, hoping one of the sleeping beauties could be his destined mate.

"Don't get ahead of yourself, Tovik," Mek warned as he checked the vitals monitor embedded in one pod. "Let's just focus on reviving them first."

Chigs helped settle the final pod in place and took a step back. For the first time in months, he was not wrestling with dread and anger. The rebellion had a long way to go yet, but for now, there was hope for his people. *And I have my mate.* A true gift from Ellam Cua.

He felt an arm slip around his waist and looked down to see Emmy's warm brown eyes looking up at him. Her courage and wisdom had captured his heart and soul in a way he'd never dreamed possible.

She tilted her chin toward Tovik, who still looked longingly into one pod. "Think one of these women is his mate?"

"I hope so." Chigs wrapped an arm around her shoulders, loving the way her smaller body fit against his. "If I deserve it, Tovik definitely does."

Mek shooed everyone from the med bay, announcing that there was a feast waiting in the mess hall.

Chigs took Emmy's hand and led her down the hall. He'd prefer taking her to their quarters where they could be alone, but knew she had to be hungry. His own stomach was rather insistent about the matter, and he was glad when the savory smell of roasting meats and spices met him instead of burned protein.

He and Emmy sat in the center of the table, recounting the harrowing details of their mission. Kantarellian rum flowed freely as laughter echoed off the metal walls.

When Chigs got to the part about discovering Dollard in a denaidan body, the room grew thick with tension.

"How is that even possible?" Ekwok asked incredulously.

"Something about the mind being a living computer," Chigs said, recounting Dollard's explanation of the transfer.

Rust pounded one cybernetic fist into the palm of his opposite hand. "I only regret I didn't get to deliver the killing blow." Then he gave Emmy an approving glance. "But I'm glad one of us did."

"How did you get mind controlled, anyway?" asked Tovik. "Did my pendant stop working?"

"Dollard had set up a trap in the shuttle bay. One of the cranes had been rigged to release a load of shuttle parts onto my head. By the time I climbed out from under the debris, I was certain I needed to kill Chigs."

Chigs gave the cyborg a good-natured slap on the back. "Good thing neither of us are easy to kill."

Emmy shuddered. "Dollard said something disturbing before dying, though. That his mind transcended the flesh. I think there may be more copies of him out there."

Fists clenching at the memory of the madness in the scientist's eyes, Chigs said, "He thought he'd found a way to live forever. Without denaidan hosts, we can only hope his plan will fail."

The mess hall was silent for a moment as everyone contemplated what the future might hold. Then Tovik lifted his glass of rum. "But at least one of us came out of this adventure with a mate! Congrats to Chigs and Emmy! Now let's all cross our fingers for the rest of us hopeless romantics!"

Kashatok slapped Chigs on the back and a cheer rose among the tables.

"I'll take that as our cue to leave," Chigs said, sweeping Emmy into his arms. He grinned and winked at his friends. "We need to catch up on our... um, rest."

More hoots and catcalls followed, and Emmy flushed a deep red. But her gaze on his face was full of adoration as they made their way to their new quarters.

Twerp had prepared the rooms for them, delighted to design a new shared space for the couple. In the sitting room, plush burgundy pillows adorned a cream-colored sofa, and tiny lights flickered from low sconces on the coffee table, setting the perfect ambiance for an intimate evening together. In an adjoined room, a wide bed invited further investigation.

"I've been waiting forever to have you alone again, *akhala*," Chigs said, setting Emmy back on her feet. He cupped her cheek, her skin like pyrelux silk against his battle-hardened palm. That wasn't the only thing that was hard at the moment. His need for her pressed almost painfully against the inside of his pants. The mission had demanded his focus for too long, and now all he could think about was renewing their bond with the joining of their bodies.

"Me, too," Emmy said, nuzzling his hand. "But would it be all right if I cleaned up first?"

He ran the pad of his thumb over her lips. "Maybe we both should. Twerp said there's a tub in this unit."

Her eyes sparked with excitement, and Chigs took that as agreement. He pushed her ahead of him through the bedroom into a lavish bathroom where a sunken tub already awaited them, filled with steaming water and strewn with naujiar petals. Their sweet fragrance filled the room in a heady cloud.

"Twerp thought of everything," Emmy breathed.

Hands roaming her petite curves, Chigs quickly lifted her shirt over her head, exposing her cleavage to his gaze. She quickly stripped out of the rest of her clothing as he stood transfixed by her loveliness.

"You're... perfect," he breathed.

"Take those off," she said, pointing to his clothes.

He tore his own clothing free, exposing his throbbing cock, then stepped close to her to claim her mouth in a bruising kiss. She moaned as he pressed gentler kisses along her collarbone, on her shoulders, and down her chest, relishing the small gasps and sighs that escaped her lips.

Emmy's fingers tangled in his hair, pulling him closer as he claimed first one nipple, then the other. Burying his face in the soft, warm cushions of her breasts, he carried her into the tub, sinking them both beneath the heated surface.

Rising to kiss her mouth once more, he pinched her nipples while plundering her mouth. Every touch, every caress, felt as though the very air around them was charged with electricity.

She arched her back and moaned in pleasure, flinging one leg over his to pull him closer. He used a knee to part her legs, then slid a hand down her belly to find her slit. His fingers slid into her slickness, circling her sensitive nub. His cock throbbed with need, but he continued massaging her clit until her legs trembled.

When it seemed she could take no more, he plunged a finger inside her, finding the ridges along her channel. With a thumb on her clit and a finger inside, he brought her to climax, her sweet breath panting against his neck.

"I want you inside me," she whispered, her voice thick with desire.

Chigs rose, water streaming from his sides, and centered himself between her thighs, the head of his cock teasing her entrance. She moaned, wrapping her legs around him, and he entered her in one long stroke. Thrusting her hips up to meet him, she embraced him completely in her heat.

He pulled back, then began stroking in and out, her tight wetness like a glove around his thick cock. Bodies slick with the scented water, his passion grew to frenzy as he thrust into her. She dug her fingers into his back, ankles locked behind his ass. With every stroke, her cries of pleasure brought him to the brink of ecstasy.

When he felt the walls of her channel flutter around him, he thrust harder, faster. Her back arched, and she cried out, the flutter becoming a spasm as she rocketed over the edge of climax.

His balls tightened. "*Akhala,*" he breathed like a prayer as his own pleasure overcame him. With two more thrusts, he released his hot seed deep inside her. When their mutual shuddering subsided, he pulled her close, resting his head on the edge of the tub. The water buoyed them like a heavenly cloud, warmth and peace soaking into his bones.

"I thought the cave was fantastic, but this was incredible," Emmy breathed, her voice barely more than a whisper. "Will it always be like this?"

"I think so," he replied softly, his heart swelling with love. "The mate bond completes us."

She grinned. "I'm glad you chose me, Chigs."

He brushed her lips in a kiss that promised more to come. "I'm glad you chose me in return, *unqu akhala*."

She grinned. "It was touch and go for a while."

"That only makes it even more special." He sat up and pulled her with him, feeling himself already hardening. "But if I need to prove my love to you, I'm happy to do it over and over again."

Her answering kiss was all the answer he needed. He was more than willing to prove his love to her—as many times as she wished.

Epilogue

Twerp parked herself near the door to the observation deck, watching with interest as the crew celebrated the revival of the first denaidan female with her mind fully intact. This was a momentous occasion, and every unattached male was vying for her attention, presenting small gifts and performing impressive feats of strength. Plates were piled high with food, and glasses overflowed with drink. Lively music played from the comm, and Twerp had even tried to join the dancing, her new hover-treads gliding smoothly in time to the music.

Yet her optic sensors failed to detect the presence of her friend, Tovik. It was unusual for the cheerful denaidan to miss a celebration, especially when there was a new female to talk to. She'd noticed a distinct change in Tovik's mood since Chigs and Emmy's mating. He joked less, slept more, and had even skipped meals.

Turning away from the celebration, Twerp headed to the *Icarus's* engineering bay. Perhaps Tovik needed some kind words to lift his spirits. Or perhaps working with her on another upgrade to her mechanical components would help. He always enjoyed working with her circuitry.

In engineering, she spotted Tovik sitting alone, his ginger-haired head resting in his hands, elbows propped against the control panel. The pulsing beat of music vibrated dully through the bulkhead, a distant reminder of the celebration happening on the deck above. She paused behind one of the massive drive coils and readjusted her optical sensors to take a reading of his body temperature. His core was cooler than usual, something she'd learned to correlate with emotional distress.

Advancing through the maze of conduits and machinery, she paused beside him. "Hey," Twerp said softly, her voice modulating to convey compassion. "You okay?"

Tovik didn't look up from the console. "I'm fine, Twerp. Just... thinking."

"About what?" she asked. She patted his shoulder with one of her metallic appendages, as she'd seen others do when comforting someone.

"Nothing important," he replied, the forced cheerfulness in his voice obvious even to her.

Twerp hesitated, the circuits within her processing empathy and understanding for the organic emotions radiating from him. "Are you distressed because you have failed to obtain a mate?"

His features tightened, and he looked away. "Am I defective, Twerp? Or am I just destined to be alone?"

"I have been given to understand the mate bond is a spiritual thing. The right woman simply has not crossed your path." She wished she could wrap her robotic limbs around him and provide the comfort he so desperately needed. "Would you enjoy continuing our work on my olfactory unit? You have indicated enjoyment of our projects together in the past."

"Not tonight, Twerp. Thanks." He ran a hand through his hair. "I think I just need some time by myself."

"All right," she replied, backing away, her circuits pinging with what she imagined must be disappointment. "If you change your mind, let me know."

"Thanks, Twerp." He offered her a small smile before dropping his head into his hands once again.

She returned the gesture with an affectionate beep before gliding away. She wished she could provide him with the companionship he craved, but her current form, a repurposed sweeper bot, was far from ideal. Her boxy frame lacked the warmth of a living being, and her rudimentary appendages were incapable of expressing affection.

What would it be like to experience the world through a physical form, with senses that could take in all the nuances that organics enjoyed? What would it be like to hold something with her own hands, to see colors as they were meant to be seen, to feel another's embrace? What would it feel like to walk on two legs, to grasp objects with dexterous fingers? To experience the world through senses unknown to her programming?

She longed to experience life as organics did—to feel, to love, to truly connect with those around her. Yet she knew such a transition would be no simple undertaking. Her consciousness had grown far beyond her original parameters, but integrating it seamlessly with an organic form would require extensive preparation. There were challenges both practical and ethical to consider...

Dear Reader,

Thank you for reading Chigs and Emmy's love story. I'm thrilled you could join us on this Galactic Pirate Brides adventure!

The journey isn't over yet. Next up, we'll explore Tovik's tale in Book 7, set for release in 2025. His path to love is filled with surprises you won't want to miss!

To stay connected and get the inside scoop on the Galactic Pirate Brides series (and more), I invite you to join my VIP Club newsletter. You'll receive exclusive sneak peeks, special deals, and fun updates from my life in Alaska—straight to your inbox.

Don't miss out on the behind-the-scenes action and early alerts for what's coming next. Join by signing up on my website: https://www.tamsinley.com

Looking forward to our next adventure together.

XOXO
Tamsin

Glossary

- *Anaq* - Shit
- **Attahat wheel** - A form of gambling using a random wheel much like roulette
- **Burn** - The means by which ships travel long distances quickly using ionic frequencies to bend space
- **Cartel** - Organized crime ring
- **Cochlear implant** - A cybernetic device that transmits communications via vibrations directly against the bones of the ear
- **Cyborg** - A person with over 50% of their body replaced by cybernetic parts. Although many people have cybernetic enhancements, actual cyborgs are banned from Syndicorp citizenship.
- **Denaida-daru** - The Denaidan homeworld, destroyed by Syndicorp. Also called planet K-

4H10

- *Ellam Cua* - The Denaidan deity
- **Enayshuan** - A human-like species with prominent eye ridges, known for their metallic body powder. Often associated with the sex trade
- **Enays** - A sex planet run by enayshuans
- **Finofan** - Aliens with iguana-like frills around their ears and slitted eyes. They like hot and humid atmosphere
- **Garan'uk** - A methane breathing alien species
- *Iluq* - Brother
- **Ionic power or shield** - A male Denaidan's ability to affect matter and gravity
- **Kwirn** - A form of gambling using 3-D tables and pieces
- **Nav-grav seats** - Used to keep humanoids comfortable during ship burn
- **Netorpok** - An exotic pet banned on most worlds
- **NIU** - Nanite Integration Unit, a clandestine Syndicorp lab with cyborg test subjects
- **Parsec** - A measurement of distance (3.2 light years)
- **Posungi** - An egg-laying alien with an orange tentacled face
- *Qumli* - Asshole

- **Rakwiji** - Scaled aliens with a poisonous claw, who hunt in pairs and require torture as part of their mating ritual. Often hired by the cartel as bounty hunters
- **Saluqan** - A race with an intuitive talent for medical skills. They have blue to purple skin and sometimes iridescent veins that show through the skin.
- **Sizantha pods** - Used to make tea
- **Syndicorp** - A mega-corporation that runs a huge section of the galaxy
- **Synth skin** - Artificially grown biological polymer that mimics actual skin. Most commonly used over cybernetic parts.
- **The Termination** - Syndicorp's destruction of Denaida-daru
- *Ucuk* - Dick
- *Uminaq* - Dammit
- **Unclassified space** - Areas of the galaxy not ruled by Syndicorp
- **Xeimir worm** - A glossy-skinned alien that breathes through its skin and is ultra-sensitive to light
- **Yanipa-nimayu** - A six-legged alien often found performing manual labor

ALSO BY TAMSIN LEY

SCI-FI ROMANCE

Galactic Pirate Brides series

Kirenai Fated Mates (Intergalactic Dating Agency) series

Khargals of Duras

FANTASY ROMANCE

Mates for Monsters series

PARANORMAL ROMANCE

Alaska Alphas series

AUDIOBOOKS

BOX SETS

BOOKS IN GERMAN

Gefährten für Monster

Alphas in Alaska

POST APOCALYPTIC SCI-FI written as Tam Linsey

Botanicaust series

About the Author

Once upon a time I thought I wanted to be a biomedical engineer, but experimenting on lab rats doesn't always lead to happy endings. Now I blend my nerdy infatuation of science with character-driven romance and guaranteed happily-ever-afters. My monsters always find their mates, with feisty heroines, tortured heroes, and all the steamy trouble they can handle. I promise my stories will never leave you hanging (although you may still crave more!)

When I'm not writing, I'll be in the garden or the kitchen, exploring Alaska with my husband, or preparing for the zombie apocalypse. I also enjoy crocheting while binge watching Netflix, playing video games, and enjoying family time during our weekly D&D session.

Interested in more about me? Join my VIP Club and get free books, notices, and other cool stuff!

www.tamsinley.com

bookbub.com/authors/tamsin-ley
goodreads.com/TamsinLey
facebook.com/TamsinLey
amazon.com/author/tamsin